BOOK REVIEWS

"Denver broke Seirra's heart years ago. He's back in town, wanting to apologize. She's trying her best to avoid him, a last-ditch attempt to keep her secret.
This book has crime and mystery alongside a second chance romance. Denver's dad wrote a letter before his death, and it turns out to be a tearjerker. But it lights the fire that Denver needs to go get his girl."
KCassenello ~ BookBub Reviewer

"Oh!! What a story. This is a very interesting and inspiring story. True love is still there after six years. Getting Sierra to admit to the love she has for Denver is a tough one. Very good reading." ~Judith S., Amazon Reader

THE REDEEMED COWBOY'S SECRET BABY

MELODY ARCHER

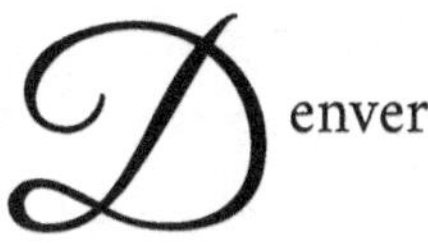enver

"So many wasted *years and wasted nights. So many years lost between us.*" Denver Callahan poured his heart out as he sang the song he'd written over six years ago.

Thousands of dedicated fans swayed to the music where they stood in the large stadium in Nashville, Tennessee.

His voice sounded raw through the microphone. Vivid memories returned of the beautiful blond who had stolen his heart.

She was the one woman whom he'd loved and lost.

Fresh anguish spilled from his lips as he sang words he'd written years ago, highlighting the pain and sadness that festered in his heart from the moment he'd first written those words until today.

Now more than six years later, this song resonated with folks all across the nation and had become his number one bestselling song.

For a moment Denver closed his eyes as he whispered the last line of the song. The music from his backup band faded away until all was quiet except for the soft strings of his acoustic guitar.

A hushed whisper fell over the crowded arena.

Denver's low voice slowly breathed out the last line of the song. *"Now I only dream of you. I don't love nobody like you."*

As his voice faded away, thousands of fans erupted into applause, the sound filling the stadium.

He grabbed his guitar and slinging the strap over his shoulder, he waved to his cheering fans as he walked off the stage.

"Man, I do believe that's the best I've ever heard you sing that song." His manager, Sid Gerrard clapped Denver on the back as he walked alongside him toward the back door of the Arena.

"Yeah? That's good." Denver's rough voice, was still raw from the painful swirling emotions of love and loss.

The stinging pain from heartbreak always hit him hardest whenever he sang that song. Tonight his vulnerable past was pressing hard into his thoughts.

"There's something so personal about that song that resonates deeply with your fans." A searching look appeared in his manager's brown eyes.

After five years of working together, Denver still hadn't told Sid all the details of how he lost the one woman he loved.

Sometimes the anguish from his loss was unbearable.

Yet, he couldn't seem to stop himself from writing all of his angsty feelings in the songs he wrote. The words and the music were a reflection of meaningful moments taken from his own life.

Denver expelled a breath and looked over at Sid with a quick nod.

As much as he appreciated his manager, he didn't want to talk about the deepest hurts lodged in his heart.

Sid seemed to understand that as he walked silently beside him.

As they walked, several members of his band echoed Sid's sentiments, congratulating him.

Denver nodded and smiled, thanking each of them for their part in pulling off another great concert. The members of his band were rock solid and an important reason why he was able to do what he did.

As he stepped out of the stadium, suddenly there was a rush of fans crowding around him.

His hired security guards stood on either side of Denver trying to protect him from the enthusiastic crowds. He looked over at the crowd glancing at them through his dark sunglasses.

Most of the fans surrounding him were college-aged girls. Each one was trying to inch forward. Some were holding up their smartphones taking pictures of him.

He sighed. As exhausted as he was from the long concert, he had made a rule for himself that he would treat people that loved his music with respect and he would honor the commitment they made to his music.

"Denver Callahan, could you please sign my copy of

your latest album?" One blond girl stepped closer to him. Seeing her light colored hair and young face, memories surfaced again of the woman he loved and lost.

His voice sounded gruff. "Sure." He quickly scrawled his name across the smooth plastic.

Suddenly she moved closer and Denver's eyes widened in surprise when she held up her phone and took a quick picture.

As soon as she stepped away, five more fans also wanted their photos taken with him.

He was grateful when his manager spoke up. "Denver only has time for another five photos, before he needs to leave." Sid pointed to five different women and men to take photos. Denver was thankful when it was finally over.

It was times like these that he was very grateful for his manager. Sid always had a way to get him out of tight spots when dealing with the crowds.

Denver wanted to leave, but since he'd already committed himself to signing music CD's and taking photos with one enthusiastic fan, he felt obligated to take pictures with others as well.

In the past few weeks he had the horrible sense that he was on a treadmill that would never stop.

Lately, Denver was desperate to get off the never-ending cycle of concerts. He was tired of having each day overseen by his publicist and manager.

He longed for greater freedom.

In the past year or so, dating a new girl in each city where he played a concert had started to lose its attraction.

It was time to take a break from this crazy hamster wheel that had become his life.

Denver expelled a breath of relief the moment his driver pulled up in the black suburban.

Jerry, his driver, hopped out and opened the backseat passenger door.

Denver stumbled into the vehicle and pulled his cowboy hat down over his face.

His manager slid onto the front seat.

"Where to sir?" Jerry got behind the wheel and looked back at him from the rear view mirror.

Denver was about to tell him to drive back to the hotel, but Sid spoke first.

"Want to go to our favorite burger joint?" Sid lifted his eyebrows, a mischievous light in his brown eyes. Denver paused a moment and nodded.

He didn't understand why his manager and friend always wanted to go out for something to eat after most concerts, but usually he went along with it.

Denver could admit he was feeling hungry. His normal routine before a concert was to have a light supper, so that he would have the energy to sing and put in the long hours performing on stage.

Adjusting his cowboy hat so it hung low enough to keep his face partially hidden, they walked into the small cafe. He really didn't want folks to recognize him. Lately, the life of being constantly in the spotlight was wearing thin.

He really needed some kind of break from all the attention he received from fans in each city he found himself in.

Maybe after this concert tour was over, he would go somewhere away from the flashing lights. He didn't know where, he just needed to disappear from the world for a little while.

The waitress led the two of them to a corner booth by the window.

Looking out into the dark streets of the late night hours, the world seemed to slow down under the street lamps that settled in around him.

Peace and quiet was just what he needed right now.

Sid ordered for him, knowing the foods he liked.

It wasn't long before the waitress came back with their coffee and burgers.

Sid grinned and eagerly took a bite out of his burger.

"Man, this is heaven."

"Yeah. This was a good idea." Denver replied and they ate in silence together for a few minutes.

As soon as Sid finished eating, he grinned. "I'm glad you agree I was right. You needed to get away and relax for a while. You should listen to me more often."

Denver nodded. A smile turned up the corners of his mouth.

"Maybe."

Sid chuckled. Many times, this was how their discussions went after a concert. Sid usually tried to talk him into something and Denver did his best to put him off.

Although, there were days — like tonight — when his manager was right about what he needed the most.

It was annoying when Sid was right.

Denver finished his hamburger and added cream to his

coffee. While he stirred, he turned his head and stared out the window as memories surfaced.

Ever since he left his small town to sing the songs he'd written to a wide audience, his life had completely changed.

He had gone from spending each day with family and friends to living many days of the year in a hotel and with his band, manager and publicist and his growing number of fans at each new concert.

At the beginning when he first started singing, it had all seemed like an exciting new adventure. It was electrifying, fun, and he loved it.

However, in the past year or so the thrill of the crowds and the concerts had begun to fade.

Even his relationship with his latest girlfriend, Jade Barlow, had fallen apart.

Jade had been angry with him when he ended their relationship.

Without warning, his smartphone beeped and as if deciphering his thoughts, a text appeared on the screen from his ex-girlfriend.

"Hey, handsome. How did the concert go?"

"Good." Denver didn't want to do this now. He texted back quickly. *"Jade, why are you texting me?"*

"I just wanted to talk to you."

"I thought we said our goodbyes last week. We agreed to stop texting and calling each other."

"Denver, saying goodbye was all your idea. I didn't want us to stop seeing each other." She wrote and then quickly sent another message. *"By the way, I just love the matching gold earrings and necklace you gave me."*

Denver sighed. "That gift was my way of making it easier to say goodbye."

"But, I don't want it to be over between us, D." He remembered Jade used that shortened nickname whenever she was trying to get her way.

This time however, it wasn't going to work.

Jade texted again. "Did you call it quits between us because I brought up the subject of marriage and children?"

Denver sighed. "You knew when we started dating that I wasn't interested in either subject."

"I'm sorry I brought it up, D. We can go back to how we were before." His ex-girlfriend added a cute emoji to her text.

But he wasn't persuaded. Not this time. "No, I'm sorry Jade. We had fun together, but it's time for us to go our separate ways."

"Aww, D. Well, maybe you'll change your mind after you've had more time to miss me. Talk to you later." She added a kissing emoji before signing off.

"Goodbye, Jade." He replied and turned off his smartphone.

He really hoped this time he had made his point and that Jade would no longer call or text him. But, he was afraid that wouldn't happen.

He knew she had a knack for being persistent when she really wanted something.

Denver set his phone down on the table feeling weighted.

Sid studied him. "Getting unwanted text messages?"

"Yeah." Denver stirred a french fry around in a circle on his plate for a moment before looking up at his friend again. "Why, can't some people understand and accept when the relationship is over?"

"Ah. That was Jade I take it?" Sid grimaced and nodded solemnly. "She must have mentioned the M or C word."

A crease formed between his brows. "M or C word?"

"Marriage or children." Sid paused for effect. "If I remember correctly, ever since you became a country music star, those two words have been taboo for any woman you've dated."

"True. And I always make sure every woman I date knows that up front."

His manager just studied him, and cocked his head to the side. "You know, Denver, someday you'll meet the woman that you can't live without. And then you'll finally need to let go of your fears, be vulnerable and give yourself permission to give and receive love."

"Yeah, yeah." There had been only one woman whom he had ever loved enough to marry.

Sierra Baxter.

She was beautiful inside and outside.

But, he'd gone and messed that up when he left town on the day of their wedding.

The memory of what he'd done had pricked at his conscience for the past seven years.

He had been young and foolish to let her go.

As he pulled his wallet from his pocket to pay for their burgers, the faded picture of him and Sierra fell onto the table.

He'd taken that photo out so many times to look at it, that the edges were faded and wrinkled from wear.

As he stared at the picture, he remembered that moment like it was yesterday.

He'd taken the picture right after she said yes to his proposal.

They had both worn matching baseball caps. Sierra had her long blonde hair up in a ponytail, leaning her head on his shoulder. He'd put the camera setting on his smartphone to camera delay and placed it along the wooden bridge railing.

The camera had snapped their picture only a few seconds later, when their heads had turned to face each other. Each of them wore sappy smiles on their faces.

He traced a finger over Sierra's smiling face, regret piercing through him like a knife.

"She's beautiful. You two look very happy together." He looked up to see the waitress' warm smile.

Denver nodded and spoke quietly. "Thanks." He handed her his credit card, wanting to hurry away.

When the waitress reached over to hand him the card reader her hand accidentally bumped the water glass and clear liquid spilled all over the picture.

"Oh, I'm so sorry." The waitress's face turned red with embarrassment and she reached over to grab a dry cloth intending to swab the photo.

"No, don't." He reached out and pulled the picture away from her reach. Water drops fell from the photo to the table, but it was still damp.

This was the only copy of the picture Denver had. He hoped the water stains wouldn't ruin the photo.

His voice sounded raw when he spoke. "I can't let this picture get messed up. I just can't."

Denver quickly paid for his meal. Grabbing his coat, he stood to his feet. He turned to look at the waitress, speaking quickly. "Sorry, but I've got to go."

He hurried out the door of the diner and over the grass to the parking lot where the suburban was parked. Hearing footsteps behind him, he turned to see Sid and Jerry, his driver following close behind.

His emotions were close to the surface especially after seeing Sierra's and his engagement photo get messed up.

All of a sudden, his belly squeezed tightly as memories of the love they shared returned full force.

"Hey man, what's the hurry?" Sid spoke in low irritated tones, as he hurried to catch up to him.

They reached the vehicle and Denver swung the passenger door open wide before looking at Sid.

"I'm just exhausted. I think it's finally caught up with me and I'm at the end of my rope. I really need to get back to the hotel and rest."

His manager held up his hands in surrender. "All right, we're going."

They all got in the suburban and Jerry drove them through traffic, arriving back at their five star Hotel in record time.

"See you all tomorrow." Denver spoke to them as he hurried toward the elevator.

"Meet me at nine o'clock sharp in the downstairs hotel restaurant. It's time to get the final details in place for your next concert. We only have a couple days left to organize things, Denver." Sid called out just as the elevator doors closed.

Denver groaned at the thought. But, his manager didn't need to worry, as he hadn't missed a planning meeting yet.

Opening the door to his suite he placed the photo of Sierra on his night table.

After a quick shower, he sank down on his bed. Maybe sleep would shake off this restlessness that surrounded him.

His thoughts were filled with ideas on how he could slow down the break neck speed of his life, when suddenly a loud ringing tone interrupted his sleep.

Waving his hand wildly in the dark, he finally landed on his phone.

"Hello." His voice was laced at the edges with sleep.

"Hey brother." Dakota's low voice came through the phone line. His brother's steady voice soothed his frayed nerves.

"Hey man." He rubbed his eyes and sighed.

"You sound a little rough around the edges. How did your concert tonight go?"

"It was great. Just tired I guess." Denver hadn't realized just how tired he really was until he'd finally crawled into his bed. But, as proven by his reaction to the water spilled on that picture, he was easily irritated and frustrated.

"You're calling after your bedtime, Dakota." He teased his brother and when he didn't respond with his usual banter, he paused. "You seem quiet all of a sudden. What's up?"

Denver knew there had to be a good reason for his brother to call this late. Usually when any of his brothers called, it was in the middle of the day because they knew his concerts went late in the evening.

His stomach knotted as a sense of foreboding filled him.

"Yeah. I called because I wanted you to hear this from me first, instead of hearing about it on the news." His brother's normally steady voice sounded pained and raw.

"Something happened to Mom or the rest of the family?" Denver swallowed quickly as his mind churned with endless possibilities.

"No, everyone in our family is fine. It's about your friend Deacon Miller's wife." Just as he was about to sigh with relief that the family was okay, Denver heard his best friend's name.

"Deacon's wife, Mary Miller? What happened?" Denver's hand shook and his grip tightened on the smartphone in his hand.

Dakota hesitated. "Mary's heart finally gave out on her. She passed away yesterday.

Denver inhaled sharply. Mary Miller passed away? "That was sudden."

"Yes it was. Mom talked with Jean Wilmer this morning. You know Mom has been in the same women's church group with Jean for years. They are all good friends." Denver remembered several women's teas at the ranch house throughout the years.

"Anyway, Jean was best friends with Mary Miller for years. Jean said Mary had been complaining about not feeling so well the last time their women's group met."

He expelled a slow breath. "Jean had tried calling Mary to talk to her yesterday. Instead, Deacon answered the phone. He told her that Mary had died in her sleep."

Denver swallowed slowly. His mentor's wife had passed away?

He had just talked on the phone last weekend with

Deacon Miller. His friend had sounded so happy and full of life. And he had spoken excitedly about his wife Mary and their plans for vacation.

Denver had first got to know Deacon and Mary Miller when he a teenager.

Deacon was a well known country music singer. He had already had a successful career before he retired with his wife to a small acreage just outside of Refuge Mountain.

He'd been a mentor to Denver. Happily talking with him and encouraging him to play and sing some of the songs he'd written.

So he would go there often after school, especially as a teenager and played guitar and sang for Deacon and his wife Mary.

Mary Miller would always tell him, the good Lord knew Deacon needed a best friend so He brought Denver into his life.

There had been a few times when Mary had seen the two of them together she voiced her thoughts with a smile. *You two are like an Oreo cookie. Each of you by yourselves are surrounded by white and dark outer skin colors but together you have a sweetness at the center that makes you irresistible to others around you.*

Denver smiled at the warm memory. His thoughts were so deep that he didn't hear his brother speak.

"Denver? Are you there?"

"I'm here." Denver stood to his feet and slipped on sweatpants over his boxer shorts.

Likely he wouldn't sleep again tonight. He paced the

length of his hotel suite, as he struggled to digest the news. His mentor's wife had passed away.

Mary had a big impact on his life.

She had been both friend and big sister to him.

When he had written and played a song about a forever kind of love, with tears in her eyes she'd looked at him.

This. You were made to do this. You were put on this earth to bring hope and happiness to people's lives with your songs.

From that moment on, Denver had committed to writing more songs with a new depth of meaning and purpose.

In high school, Denver had played guitar and sang a little in the evenings when all the ranch work was done. But, at that time in his life he didn't think playing his songs was something he could spend his life doing.

He remembered the many times Mary and Deacon had pushed him forward into his future. *Don't stop writing your songs and singing them, Denver. Heaven decided to grant you an incredible talent and it's important that you do your best to honor that gift. The two of us, we believe in you.*

Tears surfaced at the memory.

"I'm sorry, man." Dakota whispered on the phone line. His brother always had a knack for sensing how he was feeling.

Denver swallowed and whispered his voice raw and ragged. "When's the funeral?"

"In two days. Deacon Miller didn't want to wait. You should be here for that, Denver. Come home to honor your friend. Come home to see Mom. She's been talking about you more and more lately. You know Mom always does that when she's longing to see someone she loves." Dakota's words shot like an arrow straight to his heart.

He knew he should go home, but only for a short visit. "I'll come home. But, only for a few days."

"I'll tell Mom. She'll be happy to hear that." A sigh of relief was heard through the phone line.

"Good. I'll be there tomorrow."

"Sounds good, man. See you soon."

Denver turned off his phone and set it on the nearby coffee table. His thoughts still focused on Mary's passing.

Suddenly, he needed room to breathe.

Opening the sliding patio doors, Denver walked onto the balcony that was an extension of his high rise hotel suite. Leaning his arms on the railing, he looked out at the city of Nashville, his thoughts dwelling on how quickly life could end.

All of a sudden it hit him in a much deeper way than he'd ever experienced, just how short life was. A person lived and then they died.

Mary Miller had been the kind of person who had been certain of who she was and her reason for being in the world.

Denver couldn't stop the goose bumps on his forearms as he looked heavenward, remembering sweet Mary.

He whispered the words into the cool night air. "You lived your life well, Mary, giving love and kindness wherever you went."

He sighed. "I've made so many mistakes. Maybe one too many. My biggest failing, was leaving the woman I loved and was supposed to marry. I don't think that can ever be made right again."

Denver was convinced that the way he deserted Sierra years ago on their wedding day was unforgivable.

Nonetheless, he couldn't avoid going back to his hometown. He would go home to visit his brothers, his mom and to say a proper goodbye to Mary Miller.

If he saw Sierra Baxter there, he would tell her he was sorry.

However, he was convinced she wouldn't give him the time of day. She had a right to be angry and turn him away. That wouldn't be any less than he expected nor any less than he deserved.

It was time for him to go home and face the music.

DENVER LOOKED out the small side window at the night sky as his private jet taxied to stop at the Great Falls International Airport.

A knot formed in his belly as he thought of being back in his hometown of Refuge Mountain.

He'd convinced himself that it was just nerves.

But, some part of him knew it was more than that.

Regret shadowed him ever since he left town six years ago.

He could admit to feeling a little anxious at coming home.

Denver hurried down the stairs of the plane, expecting to find a taxi waiting. Instead as he turned his head he was surprised to see his brother standing there waiting for him.

"Hey man, I'm glad you decided to come home." Dakota grabbed him and pulled him into a quick hug.

His brother's embrace started a warmth in his belly that travelled the length of his body.

He was home.

Dakota pulled back and with one finger jerked his cowboy hat higher. His brother's dark eyes studied him for a moment. "It's been a few months since you were home. Glad you're back, even if it's only for a little while."

He nodded. "I didn't realize you were planning on picking me up from the airport. Thanks man."

Dakota sent him a warm smile as they both got into the pickup. "We're family, it's what we do."

His brother's words hit a raw cord inside his heart. It had been so long since someone had really cared about him without expecting something in return.

In the past few years ever since he became a country music star, it seemed everyone wanted something from him.

People were nice to him either to get access to his money or his influence.

He was tired of living in a world where almost everyone around him had some type of ulterior motive to be his friend.

"Family. It's been a long time." Denver sighed heavily. The drive back to the Callahan ranch seemed longer than usual.

His brother's dark eyes stared at him as if learning his secrets. He remembered from their growing up years that wasn't far from the truth. Dakota's ancestors from his mother's side were from the Lakota Native American tribe.

It seemed his brother had learned well from his mother's side before he was adopted by Mack and Annie Callahan.

At a deep level he knew the importance of family and had an uncanny sense about people and animals.

"It has been a long time. It's good your back home now." Dakota's smile widened as he turned the truck down the road that led to the Triple C ranch.

Bright stars shone in the night sky as they got out of the truck.

All was quiet as Denver finally found his bedroom. After a quick shower he lay down on his old bed, his thoughts returning to his mentor and the loss of his wife.

The next morning, after a restless sleep, he got up and found his way to the kitchen.

"Denver, it's so good to have you home." His mom walked toward him and pulled him into a gentle hug. He wrapped his arms around her and kissed her cheek.

"It's always good to see you, Mom." He'd been blessed along with each of his brothers that their adoptive parents had loved each of them so much.

"I feel the same way about you son. I wish we had time to have a sit down talk, Denver. It'll have to wait as the service to remember Mary's life will start soon." Mom whispered and a frown creased her brows.

"It's okay mom. I'll be here for a few days. I promise to find time for us to have a good talk."

"Thank you son."

Mrs. Garrett brought a plate of fresh muffins on the kitchen counter.

"Mom, are you ready?" Sawyer stood at the door, keys in hand.

"Yes." Annie Callahan turned to look at Denver. "See you there?"

Denver nodded. "Soon." He kissed her cheek and waved them off.

At the sound of the vehicles leaving the ranch yard, Denver picked up his back cowboy hat, slipped on his cowboy boots and headed out the door.

The entire drive to Refuge Mountain, his shoulders were tense.

He parked the old pickup truck on one of the side streets near the Community church. Folks were singing a hymn as he walked up the stairs that led into the church building.

He hesitated as he reached the landing at the top of the stairs. Instead of going inside, he sat down on the top stair, near the wood railing.

He tugged his cowboy hat farther down over his forehead as a couple of latecomers walked up the steps into the church. He would rather keep a low profile while he was back in his hometown.

Denver had the feeling most folks in this small town didn't like him much.

They didn't like it much when he had left town without marrying Sierra. He didn't blame them for that. But it did make him somewhat nervous to be back here.

Denver took off his cowboy hat as Pastor Jon said a prayer and read a few scriptures.

A twinge of discomfort washed over him as he remembered the last time he'd been in this church.

It had been the Sunday before his wedding, seven years ago. Sierra had been by his side, and everyone from their church community had been excited about the upcoming wedding day.

Sierra and he had both been happy and excited for their big day.

He'd really messed up his chance with the one woman he had ever really loved.

As the pastor began talking, Denver turned to glance quickly inside the church. He saw folks he knew. Mrs. Garrett sat with her granddaughter Cassie and beside them was his Dad's friend, old Sam.

Deacon Miller was dressed in black, seated at the front of the church near the casket of his wife. Seated nearby were a few of Deacon's friends.

Many women dabbed tissues at their eyes, as they stared at the casket at the front of the church.

Denver pinched his eyes shut for a moment at the emotional scene in front of him.

For a moment, his own memories haunted him. His birth mom had struggled as a single mom for years and finally in that last year, she had lost her own battle with cancer. He still pictured her sick and dying, seeing the images in vivid color.

Quickly, he turned his head back around, his eyes misting from the memory.

One of Deacon and Mary's good friends walked to the microphone and began sharing all the great things he had learned from Mary's life.

It was Jed Burnside who owned the Photo and Art Gallery in town.

"I always counted myself blessed the day Mary and Deacon Miller came to my store ten years ago. Mary came into the Gallery and as nervous as could be, she walked to where I stood and set a picture down on the counter. I turned the frame to see it in a better light." He paused.

"What I saw was a photograph of a sunset taken from the top of the mountain. The greenery mixed with other colors went on for miles on end. Beautiful orange, yellow and red rays of the evening sun made the sky glow around the mountains in that photo. It was stunning. I knew from that moment on that Mary's work would be on display in my gallery."

Jed took a breath and glanced down at the closed casket before looking over the crowded church. "I feel like today Mary is being shown how much her life has impacted so many people. We'll miss you, Mary."

A collective sound of agreement fell over the crowd that gathered to remember and celebrate Mary Miller's life.

Denver swallowed back tears as he thought of his friend.

Mary would've been grateful at seeing all the folks who loved her.

That's just as it should be. His thoughts were still on his friend, when suddenly the memorial service was over.

The Callahan family was one of the last to leave the church as they followed everyone over to the graveside service.

Denver arrived last, his thoughts somber as the dark clouds in the sky above.

He stood beside his brothers as the pastor spoke a few final encouraging words.

He watched as Deacon Miller and his son and extended family each placed a rose on top of the casket. They hugged each other, tears flowing unheeded down their cheeks.

Tears streamed down the cheeks of many of the people gathered there.

A woman with long blond hair wearing a black hat turned to hug Deacon.

When she turned her head, Denver realized it was Sierra Baxter.

He caught his breath.

She was even more beautiful than he remembered.

Her blue eyes were bright with unshed tears and her peaches and cream smooth skin, gave her that girl-next-door look he loved so much.

She stared at him, blue eyes shooting daggers his way. Turning, she talked quickly to her brother and Grandmother before she marched toward him.

Folks began to move away from the gravesite.

His brother Dakota shifted beside him and whispered. "I see you have someone coming your way who seems eager to talk to you. I'll see you later."

Denver merely nodded at his brother, as he focused on the beautiful woman walking his way.

Except as she walked towards him, her blue eyes flashed in anger and her lips were clamped tightly in a thin line.

"You're back." Sierra blue eyes flashed at him. As she lifted a hand to push away a loose tendril of hair from her face, her hand shook.

Denver stood still for a moment just staring at her, captivated by this woman once again.

He was tongue-tied. Seeing her again caused him to remain still. For a man who spent the last few years entertaining large crowds during his concerts, he couldn't believe one woman could bring him to his knees.

"Still not saying anything, huh?" Moisture glistened in her beautiful blue eyes, and her cheeks stained pink. "Well, you didn't say a word to me when you left six years ago, so I don't know why I imagined that would change now."

Her temper flared and she spat out the words contemptuously.

Sierra's hands fell to her hips, standing there with her blue eyes blazing in anger.

"Just do me a favor and stay away from me, Denver Callahan. You might have women in every town clamoring for a glimpse of your handsome face, but I'd rather see as little of you as possible."

With that she turned on her heel and stormed away.

A sudden pain of loss stabbed at his belly and he called after her. "Sierra, wait."

He started to go after her, but her brother Eban caught up with her. He turned to face Denver with a glare that stopped him in his tracks.

It was obvious he wasn't in Sierra's or her family's good books.

Denver stared after them as they drove away and his heart sank.

For the first time, he had a new awareness as to how much he had hurt Sierra all those years ago.

Regret rippled through each cell in his body.

How could he have just left her like that?

She had been the woman he loved. She had been the woman he was going to marry. She had been the woman he'd wronged.

He needed to do something to fix it.

He would stick around until he could have a conversation with Sierra. He needed to tell her how sorry he was for leaving years ago.

And if she didn't forgive him, well it was what he deserved.

Being near the woman who stole his heart years ago only to have her walk away would end in heartache.

He loved her still.

But, he could never make her truly happy.

He was convinced he wouldn't be a good husband. For the second time he would need to let the woman he loved go.

Any other option was unthinkable.

ierra

"Mom, are you going to come watch me play softball after school today?" Sierra's six year old son looked up from where he sat next to her at the breakfast table.

His big green eyes were large and bright, like his father's.

Seeing Denver yesterday had surprised her and brought back all sorts of memories.

She remembered the first time she'd seen Denver play guitar and sing at Rusty's Café and Bar on the edge of Refuge Mountain. She remembered when he asked her on their first date. She remembered the day he had asked her to marry him so they could spend their lives loving each other.

In spite of all those fond memories, she also recalled

the one memory that overshadowed all the others. *The day Denver didn't show up to the church on their wedding day.*

Anger pricked at her even now years later, at how he'd promised her forever and then with warning chose to take it back.

It was the reason she'd lashed out at him yesterday.

She released a long sigh, trying to let go of all those negative emotions.

Studying her son's face she smiled softly. In the end — even though Denver didn't stick around — he'd given her the best of himself, his son. She pushed back more memories of Denver that crowded into her thoughts.

Instead she focused on her son. "Of course, I'll be there sweetie."

Cody grinned. "Good. Because I want to show you how good I am at throwing the ball."

"I look forward to seeing you play, little bean." She smiled softly.

"We'll see if all those ball practices we've had here at home have helped you any." A teasing glint appeared in her brother's blue eyes and he winked at his nephew.

"Uncle Eban." Cody sighed, his lips puckering with annoyance at his uncle.

"Never mind your Uncle. He's just teasing." Grandma Baxter, spoke up from her place near the head of the table. She sat next to Granddad, helping him eat his breakfast.

Ever since his stroke three months ago, her grandfather had been weak and when he tried to talk his words came out jumbled. It had been a difficult time for all of them, but most all for her grandmother.

"I know." Cody leaned over his bowl to finish the last

few bites of his porridge. "Is Mr. Gardiner going to come and watch me play?"

"Sorry, son. He has to work late. Maybe next time."

"He's always working." Cody's face fell, his eyes sad for a moment before he glanced up with a serious expression on his face. "May I be excused from the table, Mom?"

"Yes. Wash your hands and set your backpack by the front door so you're ready to go to school, okay?" She pulled his small body close and kissed the top of his head as he passed by her.

She could hear the echo of his tiny feet hurrying to the washroom in the hallway and she smiled at the familiar sound.

Her grandmother spoke up. "Speaking of Stu, have the two of you set a wedding date yet?"

She looked across the table at her grandmother and then glanced at her brother, only to see him studying her closely.

"Not yet." Sierra swallowed. Stuart Gardiner had asked her to marry him four months ago and after three years of dating him, she had finally said yes.

"Don't keep him waiting much longer, honey. He might think you've changed your mind." Grandma had always been someone who spoke what was on her mind.

Sierra found it uncomfortable to hear the unvarnished truth.

She shifted in the wooden table chair as the truth of her words hit a little too close to home.

Her brother's brows pulled together, and his lips thinned. "Perhaps your former fiancé's arrival back in town has made you change your mind."

Sierra grimaced at her brother's sobering words. Eban didn't like Denver at all. Ever since her ex-fiancé left town years ago and she had been expecting his baby, her brother had been angry at Denver and fiercely protective of her.

She didn't blame him. After all, she had been a crying mess after Denver left town.

Eban had been the one to pick up the pieces and give her comfort when she needed it most.

He had reason to be cynical and distrusting about her former fiancé's return home.

"I haven't changed my mind. And Denver's return hasn't changed a thing. I don't expect to see him while he's home for the Thanksgiving holiday." She pushed down the fluttering in her belly as she remembered seeing him a few days ago at the funeral.

Having him back in town was almost more than she could bear. He was still as handsome as ever. His wavy brown hair and green eyes only emphasized his Italian good looks.

For better or for worse, she was still attracted to the man who proposed and then promptly left her years ago.

But, she wasn't going to give in to her attraction for that man. She refused to be taken for a ride once again.

Her fingers toyed with the spoon in her breakfast bowl before peering over at her brother and grandmother. "I was just waiting for the right time to finalize the date. I need to think of Cody also."

"Well, if you're sure." Grams looked over at her, the blue eyes that studied her were filled with questions.

Sierra swallowed and her hand shook slightly as she

raised the cup of coffee to her lips. Grandmother had always been too perceptive by half. She could see right through her and knew when something was troubling her.

She spoke more forcibly than necessary, a consuming need to convince her grandmother as much as herself. "I am sure, Grams. I've just been much too busy at the coffee shop to make any final decisions."

"Uh huh." Her grandmother's face held a deadpan look that wasn't giving anything away. Sierra knew that look.

Her grandmother was holding her cards close to her chest and not giving away what she really thought.

In the past month or so, she started having doubts about marrying Stuart. But, in the end she always talked herself back around. He was steady and predictable, which was just what her and Cody needed.

She sighed, glancing at her watch. "Well, I should get to work. It's always busy at the cafe around Thanksgiving time with all the extra visitors that love to show up to our rustic hillside village."

Sierra explained. "Mrs. Jenkins asked me to come in a little earlier today to talk, so I had better get going." She stood from the table and took her dishes to the sink.

Hurriedly, she washed her hands as she thought about the upcoming busy day.

Her grandmother walked into the kitchen, pouring herself another cup of coffee. "Did you get a chance to read the letter that came yesterday from your Aunt Serena?"

Sierra smiled. Ever since she had gone to her aunt's

hometown to give birth to her son Cody, her aunt had written one letter a month, just to catch up, she said.

"Yes, I did read it." Sierra sighed. "Aunt Serena writes that she has been thinking about coming for a nice long visit to our small town. I guess I've made the place sound very inviting in my letters."

"Hmm." Grams made a noncommittal sound. "Well, if your mother's sister is planning a long visit, I hope she doesn't mind finding a hotel in town. I've got enough to deal with over here on the farm. I'm not sure that I could add one more person to the mix."

Sierra nodded. She knew Grams didn't really like her mother's older sister for some reason. But it was true that her Grandmother had more than enough work here at home.

"I know, Grams. Don't worry, I wouldn't ask her to stay here. You have too much to take care of here at home. Now with Granddaddy sick and all, I worry about you."

Her grandmother's blue eyes moistened and she placed a calloused hand gently on her cheek. "No more worrying about Granddaddy or me. We'll be okay here."

Sierra leaned into her grandmother's soft touch loving the sense of comfort and peace she always felt when Grams was near.

"All right, no more worrying." Sierra kissed Grams cheek and grabbed her purse. She had one more thought about that letter from her aunt. "Who knows, this idea of Aunt Serena's might be another one of her flights of fancy. She might decide not to come to visit at all."

Her grandmother sighed in relief. "Well, good then. We don't need to think about that today."

"Yes, we don't need to think about that."

Cody came to the kitchen to add his lunch box to his backpack.

Eban was slipping his jacket on to go milk the cows and feed the chickens. He had taken over the large task of running the farm ever since grandfather had gotten so sick.

Her younger brother was only twenty-two and still quite young to have all that responsibility. But, he had learned well from all his growing up years of working with Granddad on the farm.

Her stomach knotted once again and she looked over at her brother. "Remember Cody has a baseball game after school. You'll stay until I can get there?"

"Yeah, no problem." Eban grabbed his cowboy hat and slipped it on his head.

Sierra's fingers tightened on her purse. "And you'll remember not to drive along Riverview road? I know the road along Hillside drive takes a little more time, but it's safer especially after the rain and cold weather we've had lately."

Eban sighed heavily. "I'll remember." Her brother squeezed her hand. "It'll be okay. We'll be safe."

Tears pricked the back of her eyes at the understanding in her brother's eyes. He also was haunted by memories of the Thanksgiving weekend when their parents had died in a car accident years ago.

Sierra had been five years old and Eban just three years old when it happened. They had been devastated and heartsick.

That was when she and her younger brother had gone

to live with Grandma and Grandpa Baxter on their farm located only a few miles outside of Refuge Mountain.

Her grandparents had raised the two of them with a lot of love and care, but there was still a large hole in her heart at the loss of her parents.

Blinking back the tears, Sierra nodded quickly and squeezed her brother's hand. "Thanks. I know you will."

She turned and seeing her grandmother, she kissed her weathered cheek. "Thank you for breakfast and for always looking out for all of us. You're the best. I love you, Grams."

"Oh darlin', I love you too. Have a good day today and no worrying, all right?" Grams reached up and touched her cheek with one hand, as she looked carefully into her eyes.

Sierra smiled. "I'll do my best."

She gave a quick hug to her grandmother and saw Cody waiting at the front door as usual. Sierra walked over to him and kneeled on the kitchen floor, looking directly into his wide green eyes.

"I look forward to seeing you play ball after school, little bean. But, for now I'd better get going to work." She smiled and her son returned a wide smile as he threw his chubby arms around her neck.

She pulled him into a close embrace, happy that he was still at an age where he was openly affectionate.

"I love you, Mom."

She kissed his cheek and whispered. "I love you too, son. See you later."

With one last wave to everyone, she headed out the front door to her old blue car. She was grateful to her brother for starting it ahead of time, so she could feel a little warmth from the heater.

As usual she took the long windy road filled with potholes instead of the newly paved and much shorter highway that led towards their country township. Parking her little blue car behind *The Little Bean Cafe*, she hurried inside.

"Look what the wind blew in." Mrs. Jenkins smiled as she carried a coffee pot in one hand. "It's a little chilly today. Better come in and warm up by the fire."

Sierra closed the door and hurriedly took her jacket off and hung it up on the coat rack in the small back room of the cafe.

She walked to the front and joined her boss behind the front counter.

Sierra looked around at the log walls and rafters inside the coffee shop. There were painted wooden toys that sat on ledges on three walls. Some were horses, dogs, cattle and even some antique cars that one of the local craftsmen had carved out.

A couple of swirling green vines stretched along the tall walls, adding that homey look visitors said they adored every time they entered the cafe.

Mrs. Jenkins grabbed her oven mitts and pulled out a batch of Saskatoon berry muffins from the over. Smiling, she breathed in the scent of her favorite muffins.

"You want a cup of coffee, Mrs. Jenkins?"

"Of course. We still have a good bit of time before folks start coming in, so we can enjoy a nice cup of coffee." Mrs. Jenkins winked at her and buttered a hot muffin for each of them. Setting the coffee and muffins on a tray, she carried it over to the table that was near the fireplace.

Sierra poured a cup of hot coffee for each of them, adding the cream they both liked and went to join her boss.

For a moment they each sat quietly enjoying sipping their coffee while listening to the sounds of the fire crackling merrily, adding to the cozy atmosphere.

Lottie Jenkins sat in the cushioned chair across from her, watching the fireplace. Sierra had worked for Lottie ever since she started High School and had really come to love this place and the people who came through the doors each day.

The coffee shop was located in a quaint little spot on the corner of Main Street where many folks in Refuge Mountain found themselves meeting old friends or making new ones.

Sierra really liked feeling like she was part of the community. Many people from their neighborhood had supported her in many different ways.

She was grateful to them.

"Most likely you're curious why I asked you to come in to work early." Lottie Jenkins' words broke the silence, disrupting Sierra's thoughts. Her boss's brown eyes studied her carefully before she went on.

"I am." Sierra took a bite of the muffin, savoring the way it melted in her mouth. In fact, she had been sort of worried. Was her boss about to lay her off of work?

"I've been thinking a lot about how busy this coffee shop has become and realized in the past year or so, it's been more difficult for me to keep up with it all. I'm not getting any younger. To top it off, I have started to feel tired and sore at the end of each day's work. Putting it plainly, I'm getting too old for this."

"You're not old, Lottie." Sierra sipped her coffee, looking over the rim at her boss. Sure, Lottie Jenkins short wavy hair was completely grey now and there were wrinkles near her eyes, but those were smile lines.

Mrs. Jenkins had been so generous to her ever since she started at *The Little Bean Cafe*. Sierra hardly noticed little details like wrinkles anymore, because she had been so impacted by the kindness of her boss's heart.

Lottie held up her hand. "I am blessed that you don't see me as old my dear. But, the truth is I am beginning to feel my age. Besides, now that I am seventy, I realized there are a few more adventures I still want to be part of and less time to do them."

"Are you needing a vacation?" To Sierra it sounded like her boss needed a break.

Lottie laughed lightly. "A rather long one, as it turns out. My plan is to sell the place."

Sierra choked on her coffee, setting the cup on the coffee table between them. She looked over at her boss, and sputtered out the words. "Sell *The Little Bean Café?*"

"Yes. It's time. Which is why I wanted to talk to you first."

"Okay." Sierra could feel knots forming in her stomach as she worried about these new changes that would be coming.

Lottie took another sip of her coffee, before she turned toward her, her gaze studying her before she spoke again. "It's been a few years since you mentioned an interest in buying this coffee shop. So, I thought I'd double check. Are you still interested?"

Sierra exhaled the tension that had been building inside her. It took her a moment to get her head around what her boss was saying.

"Still interested?" She chuckled. "Yes, I am. I've always loved this place, but I'm just not entirely sure if I can afford it. What's your asking price?"

She thought of the money she'd been saving from every paycheck for the past four years. Most likely she didn't have enough savings for the down payment but perhaps she could see what sort of options were available for business loans.

"Here's what I'm thinking. Remember, this price is only being offered to you." Her boss winked at her. "In the past year I've had several offers already from development corporations from big cities, who want to buy up a string of buildings especially on the main street of our village."

She paused. "But, I would rather sell this to someone who will love the place and the people of this town as much as I do. Someone like you, Sierra." She pulled a piece of paper and pen from her pocket and quickly wrote down a number.

Mrs. Jenkins handed the paper to Sierra. "That's what I'd like for the place. What do you think?"

Sierra swallowed as she saw the large six-figure number. It was a lot of money, yet she knew Lottie had already offered her a reduced price.

She glanced up with a shaky smile at her boss. "This is very reasonable. I realize you could get a whole lot more for this Café. I do have money in savings that has been adding up over the years, but I'll also need to try to work out a loan. If I can figure out the financing, I will be happy to buy the coffee shop from you, Lottie. I can think of nothing I'd like more."

Lottie Jenkins grinned brightly. "Good, I'm glad to hear it. And let me know how the financing with the bank goes. We'll do our best to figure this out."

Sierra nodded, her smile a little shaky. "Yes. I will let you know."

"Good." Lottie stood to her feet and held out her hand.

Sierra shook Lottie Jenkins hand, a wide smile on her face. "Thank you for talking to me first."

"Of course." Her boss looked at the clock on the wall above the large wooden door. "Looks like it's time to open up. We'd better get on with the day's work. Our regular customers will be walking through that door any minute ready for their coffee."

Sierra went over and unlocked the front door and before long was serving a continual flow of customers.

She was just pulling a fresh batch of baked muffins out of the oven, when she heard the voice of her fiancé.

"It's good to see you, Sierra." She turned around to see Stuart standing at the front counter, his hands busy pulling lint off the front of his navy blue suit jacket.

"You too, Stu. Are you staying for lunch today?" She set the muffins on the warming rack near the stove and turned to him.

"Sorry, I can't today. I've got a meeting. You're keeping busy." He looked around the Café with a shaky smile. Belatedly, she remembered how he never liked large crowds.

"Yes, we've had a steady crowd of folks ever since we opened up this morning. But, this is normal for Thanksgiving week." Sierra poured a coffee and handed it to Stuart.

"Thanks." He turned to her. "I'll take my usual lunch to go."

"Sure. I'll only be a moment." She busied herself making his pastrami on rye with pickles on the side. It was the same sandwich he had everyday. He also arrived at the coffee shop at the same time everyday.

Predictable and steady, that was Stuart's way.

She handed him his food and asked. "Are you sure you can't make it to Cody's baseball game after school today? It would mean so much to him." It would also mean a lot to her, but she didn't add that part.

He sighed. "No, I can't, Sierra. I'm really sorry but I'm swamped. Getting this work finished is too important. I don't want to lose this client as I'm fairly certain this project will qualify me for a big promotion."

Disappointment burned like a festering wound in her belly. Not once in the past year had Stuart showed up for anything that was important to her son. She wanted to tell him how unfair that was, but they were in a public place and she didn't want to get into it with him now.

"All right then." She sighed heavily. "Will we still see you for Thanksgiving dinner?" It seemed because her fiancé continued to not show up to important events, she was now doubting he'd keep other commitments.

"Of course. I'll be quite happy to eat your Grandmother's good cooking." Stuart smiled as held up his wrapped sandwich. "Thanks again. I'll see you later."

"Sure." Sierra nodded, her gaze following him as he left the coffee shop. She tried to tamp down the gnawing sensation that gripped her belly. Why was she suddenly having doubts about her relationship with Stuart?

This was what she signed up for when she agreed to marry him. She knew he was busy in his career as an accountant. *Remember, Sierra, you like the fact that he is predictable and safe. He feels steady, he wants a family and he has lived in this rural township for years. This is what you wanted.*

She reminded herself of what she believed she wanted when she first started dating Stuart.

Dating Stu meant that everything was very neat, orderly and safe. She reminded herself that was what she signed up for when she'd said yes to his proposal. Based on past experience, life was filled with too much pain and sometimes those you loved abandoned you without warning.

The memory of Denver not showing up for their wedding and the sting of that betrayal haunted her still.

It was a good reminder of why she had chosen to marry a very different man. A man who was steady and who wanted a family was a much better choice.

These thoughts swirled around in her head off and on throughout the day, until her co-worker Avery showed up for her late afternoon and evening shift at the coffee shop.

Avery had recently graduated from High School and was working at the coffee shop to save money for college. She was a good worker and fun to be with.

"Are there special orders I need to know about?" Avery

tied an apron around her waist, her dark brown eyes glancing in her direction.

"Not for tonight. Your shift should be worry free." Sierra grinned at her co-worker. Every worker at the Café knew there wasn't any shift that was completely free from worry. Yet all employees at *The Little Bean Cafe* were prepared for special orders that were occasionally requested by folks in their small town.

Bulk orders of baked goods or specialized coffee were usually requested by customers when they had special meetings or events planned. It was a lot of extra work to put together a large order.

"Okay, good."

Sierra took off her apron and hung it up.

She slipped on her coat and grabbed her purse.

Her boss called out as she started to leave. "Have fun at the baseball game. Tell Cody I'm cheering for him."

"I will. See you later." Sierra waved to her boss and headed out the back door.

She drove her small car to Refuge Mountain's baseball field.

Her son's Little League game was just getting started as Sierra stepped onto the bleachers to find a spot to sit.

Stepping past other parents and grandparents who were cheering on their children or grandchildren, she made her way to where her brother sat on the bleachers.

"You made it."

She grinned at her brother and bumped his shoulder with hers. "Of course. I'm determined to watch my son's games. I want Cody to know how important he is to me."

"Too bad your fiancé doesn't see things the same way."

Sierra sighed heavily. "I wish Stu was here. He's busy working overtime for an important client. He says if he does this job well, it's likely he'll be given that promotion he's been longing for."

Eban shook his head slightly and grimaced.

"I know, you're thinking that's not likely. But maybe, Stu will have more time after he has finished this project."

She stared out at the baseball diamond, not really believing her own words.

"I didn't say a word. But for yours and Cody's sake, I really hope that's true."

She nodded and whispered sadly. "Me too."

Before long, Cody was up to bat. Sierra stood to her feet, a grin on her face.

Her son swung at the first ball from the pitcher, but missed. He was luckier the second time around, as his bat connected with the soft ball with a loud thud. Cody ran to first base, keeping his foot on first base just like his uncle had taught him.

Sierra and Eban were both cheering him on as the next player went up to bat. The boy hit the ball even farther and Cody managed to make it all the way to home base before any of the players on the bases were able to tag him with the ball.

"Good run, Cody." Sierra cheered her son, who looked up toward the bleachers with a happy grin on his face.

"He's doing well. Maybe we'll have a professional base-ball player in the family someday." Eban grinned at her as the next batter stepped onto the mound.

"He sure loves to play ball." They cheered on the team

until the last inning finished. Cody's team won only by a few points, but they were happy.

Eban whispered in her ear. "Have you had a chance to let Denver know that he has a son?"

Sierra looked at her brother and shook her head. She whispered. "No." She was scared of what his response would be to the news, even though she realized telling him was the right thing to do.

"Well, you'll want to tell him soon, before he finds out from the local gossip mill." Eban looked beyond her and whispered.

"No one knows who Cody's father is, other than you, Aunt Serena, Granddaddy and Grams. So, I don't know what the gossip mill would have to say." Sierra had done her best to protect her family from unwanted gossip. Up until a few months ago when Cody started school, her son had stayed at the farm most of the time, so he'd been protected at home.

Sierra had tried many times to contact Denver when she was pregnant, but he hadn't responded.

Her brother whispered. "They don't need to speak the truth, Sierra. The reason they're called gossip mills is because they are spreading false assumptions and lies about you or your son."

Sierra visibly shuddered. "Well, if folks want to speak lies about me, I guess they can go ahead. But, you're right. I do need to tell Denver about his son and soon."

Eban looked at the other end of the bleachers and nodded. "Well, here's your chance because he's headed this way."

Sierra turned, the blood seemed to rush out of her head and down to her toes.

As their eyes met, she felt a shot run through her. She barely heard her brother whisper. "I'll go take care of Cody and bring him home."

"Okay, thanks." Sierra whispered back but her eyes were glued to Denver Callahan.

Denver walked up onto the bleachers, followed by his brother Wyatt and sister-in-law Abby and their two adopted boys, Joey and Tony. Wyatt and Abby got stopped mid-way talking to one of the ranchers in the area, but Denver made a beeline straight for Sierra.

She stood motionless.

Folks around her stood to their feet and talked amongst themselves, but she couldn't seem to move. Her gaze was glued to Denver's green eyes that focused intently on hers.

Even though his eyes were slightly shadowed by the black cowboy hat slung over his forehead, she could make out the familiar intense look that had always seemed reserved especially for her.

Denver came to a stop directly in front of her.

"You're still here." Sierra knew her voice held an accusation. But, she couldn't help it. She was still angry with him.

His green eyes held an intense light to them that caused her to squirm a little.

He nodded. "It is Thanksgiving." His eyes glittered and he stepped even closer.

She could hardly be upset that the one man she hoped

would leave town right away, was staying to visit his family for Thanksgiving.

Still, she couldn't help but wish he would leave.

The sooner the better.

Sierra was just about to respond, when a voice called out their names. "Oh, Denver Callahan, you are still here. Just the man we wanted to talk to." Mrs. Mabel Moore walked in between the stands, followed closely by Mrs. Dorothy Spaulding.

Both women were a little out of breath by the time they reached them.

"Hello, ladies." Denver turned, not missing a beat. Sierra sighed. She imagined he was quite used to women unexpectedly calling out his name. Mostly likely he got that all the time as a famous country music star.

Mabel Moore turned to her, a sly smile on her face. "Sierra, it's nice to see you too." She turned to glance at Dorothy Spaulding who stood beside her. "In fact, seeing you both is perfect. The two of you are just the people we need to talk to."

Dorothy Spaulding smiled brightly and nodded, the dimples on her cheeks creating deep grooves in her cheeks.

A crease formed between Sierra's brows as she studied the two women. The two of them sat on the town council of their small town and were always trying to involve more folks from the town in their plans.

"Why do you need to talk to both of us?" Sierra was beginning to have a niggling in her belly that the two women were up to something.

"Well, all the folks on the town council were so excited

that you agreed to host our Annual Christmas Fair, Sierra. But then we got to talking, just this past week as a matter of fact." Mabel Moore looked from Sierra to Denver as she continued.

"We were thinking, wouldn't it make the Christmas Fair even better if there was someone who could co-host this event alongside Sierra?"

Sierra bristled a little on the inside.

What were they thinking? Did they think she needed Denver's help?

"I'm perfectly capable of hosting Refuge Mountain's Christmas Fair. We already have it all planned out. I'm ready to go for Monday." Sierra smiled at Mrs. Moore, offering her most confident smile.

Mrs. Moore replied. "Oh I know you'll do fine, my dear. But, I think adding a well known country singer that was raised in our very own Refuge Mountain, would be just the thing to draw the crowds."

The older lady eyed Denver. "Your mother mentioned that you were home for Thanksgiving, and that you might be willing to help us out. What do you say, Denver?"

Heat burned her neck and slipped upwards toward her cheeks. How could these ladies change things up like this unexpectedly?

She didn't want to co-host the Christmas Fair with her former fiancé. The only hope she had left for any peace of mind was that Denver would say no.

She turned to him and saw the corners of his mouth turn up in amusement.

"Well, ladies, I hadn't planned on staying here in my old home town longer than for the Thanksgiving holiday.

As much as I would like to take you up on your offer to spend more time with Sierra, I will have to decline. Maybe, there will be another time when I'll be free to say yes."

Sierra's eyes grew big and round as Denver smiled his rogue smile at her. It was the same smile that years ago made her knees weak.

If she were completely honest, he still affected her strongly, but Sierra did her best to hide how vulnerable she was to him.

She sputtered a little at his bold gaze.

He studied her face until it felt like he'd touched her. "In fact, I hope there will be another opportunity, as I believe I would really like to spend more time with this beautiful lady."

His honeyed tones as well as his intense green eyes caused a fluttering warmth in her belly.

Sierra shifted uncomfortably at Denver's blatant stare.

She looked over the two women in an effort to deflect the attention off of her.

Both women's faces fell. "Well, we tried." Mrs. Moore shook her head as she glanced at Mrs. Spaulding. Turning to Denver once more, she said. "However, in case you change your mind, the offer will be open, Denver."

"Thank you lovely ladies. I'll keep that in mind."

Sierra didn't like the fact that these ladies from the town council kept their offer open. It made it too easy for Denver to change his mind.

She tucked her hair behind her ears, suddenly uneasy at the thought that Denver might stick around town.

Not only was she worried over her obvious strong

attraction to her former fiancé but, she was more worried about the big secret she hadn't shared with him yet.

Without warning, she heard Stuart's voice calling her name. "Sierra, there you are. I decided you were right. I have been spending too much time at work. So I came to the baseball game, but I'm afraid I didn't make it in time to see…"

Sierra quickly interrupted before he could say her son's name. "…to see your favorite game. Well, that's okay. You can always catch the next one." Her heartbeat accelerated, going ninety. "Stu, we should get going."

"Wait. Aren't you going to introduce me to your friend, Sierra?" Denver cut in looking at Stuart with that tough assessing stare she remembered so well.

Her heart pounded louder in her ears. Well she might as well get it over with. "Sure. Stuart Gardiner, I'd like to introduce you to Denver Callahan." She looked at Denver and squared her shoulders back, speaking with a resolve she didn't feel inside. "Stuart is my fiancé."

Denver's eyes flickered with something similar to irritation.

"Fiancé huh?" Her former fiancé's green eyes narrowed as he looked at the man by her side.

Stuart wore his blue suit jacket with a light brown sweater under it and tan dress pants. His blond hair was styled in the latest hairstyle. He was always presentable and precise, that was Stuart's way.

Sierra could sense the wheels turning in Denver's mind and it wasn't in Stu's favor. "What do you do for a living?"

Stuart seemed only vaguely aware of the emotional

undercurrents, as he was always happy to talk about himself. "I'm an accountant at Bittman and Witticombe here in town. I'm hoping to become a partner soon."

Denver's expression was one of pained tolerance as Stuart continued to talk in detail about his job.

Sierra's mouth quirked up in amusement.

She knew Stuart wouldn't make a big fuss about Denver's country star status, as Stu didn't even listen to country music. Most likely he'd never listened to any of Denver's music albums.

It would be good for Denver to finally talk to someone who didn't fawn over him like most of his fans did.

"Sounds like you're busy."

"Yes. In fact, Sierra is always asking me to take more time away from work." Stuart slipped an arm around her waist and pulled her closer. He turned to her with a big smile. "I think she just wants a lot more of my company."

Denver's square jaw tensed visibly at the gesture.

Sierra could sense her former fiancé was getting ready to give Stu a piece of his mind.

She took a step back, hoping that it would signal to Stuart that she was ready to go. "It was nice talking with you, Denver. We need to go. Happy Thanksgiving." Sierra forced a smile and walked away with Stuart hurrying to catch up.

She didn't dare look back at Denver.

The entire time she stood next to him, she had been increasingly aware of her attraction to him. Any appeal her former fiancé had in her eyes, needed to be stopped now.

It wasn't right, seeing as how she was engaged to another man.

As Stuart walked her to her car, she noticed his set face, clamped mouth and fixed eyes. "You didn't tell me your old fiancé would be here at the ballgame."

Stuart's cynical remark grated on her.

"I didn't realize he would be." Her lips thinned in irritation.

There was a long brittle silence before he spoke again. "Have you told him yet that he has a son?"

Sierra hadn't given Stuart many details of her relationship with Denver. She'd made it plain to Stu that she didn't want to continually be reminded about the first man she had agreed to marry. She wanted to live in the present and yet she knew if she married Stu, she would need to explain everything.

However, today his questions felt more like an interrogation.

Sierra forced herself to smile. "No, I haven't. There hasn't been time. I will tell him, I'm just trying to figure out the right time."

"Well, you should probably do that soon."

Sierra nodded and stepped closer to her car. "I will."

Stu hesitated and then spoke with an edge to his voice. "Well, I don't like the way he looks at you. I think he's still attracted to you and wants you back."

She heard the irritation in his tone of voice. "Stu, you don't have anything to worry about. He doesn't want me back. This is the first time I've seen him in a long time. Besides, he's leaving after Thanksgiving weekend."

Stuart was quiet for a moment as he digested this news. He sighed. "I hope so."

He studied her with an apologetic gaze. "I'm sorry, Sierra. I was jealous. Forgive me?" Stu's tone was remorseful and resigned.

"I do forgive you. Let's not think about Denver. He's just an annoyance that will soon be out of our lives."

"You're right as usual." He put his arms around her and held her close for a moment. Placing a light kiss on her cheek he stepped back. "I'll see you tomorrow for Thanksgiving dinner."

Sierra opened her car door and nodded. "Good. Grams will have a lot of food, so make sure you're hungry."

"I will." Stu laughed and waited until she was in her car before turning and walking to his vehicle.

As she drove back home, Sierra couldn't help but feel troubled by the fact that Stu doubted her relationship with Denver. Hanging onto doubt and jealousy wasn't a good way to start a marriage.

Besides he was wrong about Denver being attracted to her. He was just being his usual bothersome self.

She could admit that she was still attracted to Denver, but nothing was going to happen because she didn't date around when she was committed to one man. Besides, it was a moot point since he was leaving soon.

However, the fact remained that sooner rather than later she would need to have that talk with Denver.

Grams had reminded her the other day: *The chickens will come home to roost sooner than you think. They always do. So darling, you'd better tell Denver about his son before you regret it.*

Sierra promised she would tell Denver about his son. And she'd do it soon.

CHAPTER THREE

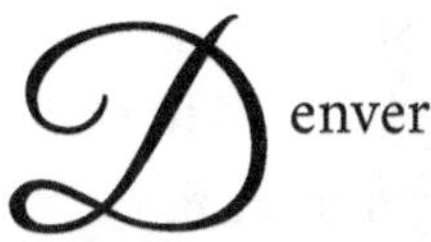enver

"I'M SO happy you could be home for Thanksgiving dinner, Denver, and that you could stay the holiday." His mom looked over at him from her place at the head of the table, a gentle smile on her face.

She reached over and squeezed his hand.

"Ah, mom. I know it's been too long since I've been home, but I am always happy to see you." Denver turned to see the rest of his family around the dining room table. His brother Wyatt was smiling down at his new wife Abby, his face glowing with love for her.

As he studied the two of them together, he was reminded of the moment he saw Sierra yesterday at the baseball game.

His heart accelerated just thinking of her.

Sierra was even more beautiful today than she'd been six years ago when he'd asked her to marry him. However, seeing her on the arm of another man yesterday had sparked a possessive anger on the inside that shocked him.

Denver realized with startling clarity that he was still attracted to the first woman he ever loved. The admission was dredged from a place beyond logic and reason.

All these past few years of telling himself that he didn't want to fall in love, came back to mock him.

And now Sierra was going to marry another man.

He was too late.

His heart squeezed painfully in his chest.

Denver took a sip of water, and forced himself to smile at his brothers who were joking and laughing around the table.

"Brother, at long last you're home." Cole, his youngest brother teased him. "It's good to see you."

"And I suppose I can stand the sight of you too Cole and all these other Callahan's too. Excluding my new beautiful sister-in-law of course. It's always lovely to see you, Abby."

Abby grinned and looked at her husband Wyatt. He simply smiled and sipped his coffee.

Cole grinned. "Well, how do you think all of us feel being forced to look at you?"

Denver grinned. "Ah, it's nice to be at home again where I am truly appreciated."

His brothers chuckled at the irony they heard in his voice.

The rest of his brothers started talking and cracking

jokes. His heart warmed at the feeling of home and the connection to family he always felt here.

Annie Callahan took a sip of her hot cup of tea and set it down.

She turned to Denver with a sudden smile. He didn't know what to think of the mischievous look he saw in her eyes.

"Mrs. Moore called me yesterday. She was disappointed that it didn't work for you to co-host the annual Christmas Fair on the local television show with Sierra Baxter."

Denver cocked his head to the side. "I'm sorry. I hope that won't cause problems. My plan is only to be here for a few days, so I wouldn't be able to help them out for the time they need me. From what I understood from Mrs. Moore, you mentioned that I might be available to help her out."

A rose color blossomed in his Mom's cheeks and she grimaced. "I'm sorry, son. I shouldn't have gone ahead and told Mabel you might be willing to co-host the show. But, at the time it seemed so right. I couldn't help myself."

Denver folded his arms across his chest. "Uh huh." His green eyes narrowed a fraction as a thought crossed his mind. "This doesn't have anything to do with the woman who was already asked to host the show does it?"

"Maybe." Annie Callahan had the grace to blush prettily. She looked over at him and sighed. "All right. I don't know what to tell you, Denver. I've always adored Sierra Baxter."

His mother sighed. "I haven't seen her much since you left town, but every once in a while I stop in at *The Little*

Bean Cafe and see her beautiful face and I think of how good things could have been for the two of you if you would have married."

The memory of seeing Sierra yesterday returned. He had been drawn to her like a moth to a flame. He was more attracted to her now then he'd been six years ago when he'd asked her to marry him.

That scared him.

A surge of sorrow mixed with anger swept over him. His biggest regret in life was that he'd left her. He was at fault because he didn't stay here in his hometown and make Sierra his wife.

Instead he'd left to follow the sudden opportunity he'd been given to chase his dream as a country singer and songwriter.

Looking back, he regretted that hasty decision.

Seeing the woman he once loved enough to marry, reminded him of just how much he had lost.

When he'd seen the man Sierra agreed to marry by her side, anger had flooded him and he'd wanted to deck the guy. He wasn't normally an aggressive man, but seeing Sierra with a new man by her side — a man she loved enough to marry — caused his blood pressure to rise.

Now, even after all these years his mom still held onto the hope that he would marry Sierra.

Since she was engaged, it didn't look like that wasn't going to happen.

"Mom." Denver sighed heavily. "It's been too many years and too much water under the bridge."

"Maybe. But again, maybe not." His mom leaned closer, her gaze intent on his. "However, I think you owe it to yourself to find out. Who knows, your Dad might have had the right idea about love and second chances when he wrote you and your six brothers that letter before he passed away."

Moisture filled her eyes and she tried to blink it away. "Maybe now that you're home for a little while, this would be a good time to read that letter again, son."

Denver sighed, knowing he wasn't going to win this conversation with his Mom.

A surge of guilt knotted his belly.

He still hadn't read his father's last words. After the funeral he had stuck the letter in an old book and left it there. Well, he supposed there was no time like the present.

"I will read Dad's letter again, Mom. But, please do me a favor. Promise me you won't meddle in my love life any more, all right?"

She nodded and whispered. "I promise. I love you, son."

"I love you too, Mom." Denver offered her a reluctant smile. He loved his mother and no matter how many times she interfered in his personal life, he always forgave her.

He knew she loved him and meant well.

However, ever since his dad passed away, she had been on a mission to see all her sons married to the women who had been their first love.

"Will you be sticking around the ranch for a while, Denver?" Wyatt sat on the couch with his arm around Abby, while their two adopted boys Joey and Tony played a game of chess with their uncles Dakota and Hunter.

Denver squirmed a little both inside and outside. He was glad to see his brother and his new wife so devoted to each other. For some reason he couldn't help but have a strong sense he was missing out on a lot by not being in a similar relationship.

He stuffed down his feelings as he'd done for the past six years. "No, I'm heading back early next week again. Sid has the next concert tour already planned out."

"Well, the best laid plans and all that. But for what it's worth, I was hoping you would stay home for a while longer. You look like you could use a rest." A crease formed between Wyatt's brows as his brother studied him.

It seemed his oldest brother had subtly taken over his Dad's role of checking on how each of the family was doing.

It came naturally to Wyatt to take care of family or animals. That explained why his brother had studied Veterinary medicine in College. He had a need to see that all living things around him were taken care of.

"I guess." Denver sighed and looked down at the smartphone in his hand and saw the messages he'd listened to earlier. "But that might need to be put on hold as I have to get back on the hamster wheel of the next concert tour soon. My manager has already left me messages."

"You could always tell him you need a break."

Wyatt's words were a stark reminder of his goal to slow down and to live on the land he inherited from his Dad in the quiet shadow of the mountains.

All he wanted was to hide from the non-stop fans and

people wanting his attention for a good long while. He longed for peace and quiet.

But, before he could do that, he needed to apologize to Sierra. He knew he would have no peace of mind until he did.

His brother studied him, and Denver squirmed uncomfortably.

He forced a half smile and shook his head. "Yeah, as much as I'd like to do that, I don't know if that can happen anytime soon."

Mrs. Garrett walked into the great room carrying a tray of coffee and tea, which she set on the side table. "Something to warm you on this chilly day."

"Thank you, Mrs. Garrett. You take such good care of all of us. And thank you again for another delicious Thanksgiving dinner." Annie Callahan smiled over at their cook. Their cook had been a good friend as well as a necessary part of their family all these years.

"Happy you all liked it. And speaking of the Thanksgiving meal, there were a lot of leftovers. Is there any family in particular you would like me to give the leftover food to, Mrs. Callahan?" Mrs. Garrett finished pouring hot tea and handed it to his mom.

His mother looked at him for a moment before turning back to talk to their cook.

"Wait for a little while. Let me talk to Denver."

"All right. I'll go pack up the food."

His mom turned to Denver, as their cook left the room.

"Denver, I have an idea."

"I'm listening."

"You know how each year we give the leftover food to someone in our community." He nodded. Ever since he was adopted into the Callahan family, his mom had always had their leftover Thanksgiving and Christmas dinners boxed up to give to different folks in the community.

His mom continued in a soft voice. "Well, this year I thought we might send the meal to Deacon Miller. With the recent loss of his wife, perhaps it would encourage him to know someone is thinking of him. I was thinking, you might like to bring it to him."

His mom's gaze searched his. Denver never could say no to his mom when she looked at him with those soul-filled blue eyes.

"All right, I will. I haven't talked to him much since he lost his wife, so it would be good to see him." Denver nodded. He stood to his feet and turned when his Mom spoke once again.

"One more thing, son. Would you take your guitar? I think hearing you sing some of your songs would cheer him more than anything."

Denver thought of all the years since he was a teenager, and how he spent so much time with Deacon Miller. The man had been a well known country singer and songwriter.

As a teenager, he had often stopped by his house after school and Mr. Miller would ask Denver to play any new songs he had written.

He had seen him recently at his wife's funeral, and Deacon Miller had looked weary and frail.

It would be good to talk with him again.

He nodded to his mom and spoke to the family. "Be back later." Denver lifted his hand in a quick wave and hurried to his old room to grab his guitar.

He changed into a pair of western style jeans and picked up his guitar and put it in the case. He walked to the door, when he turned his head and spotted an unopened envelope.

It stuck out a couple inches out of a favorite book his adopted father had loved to read, the true life story written by pioneering rancher Richmond P. Hobson titled *Grass Beyond the Mountains*. His Dad had always loved cowboy stories that he could relate to.

After Mack Callahan had passed away a little over a year ago, he remembered receiving the letter his Dad had written.

He had left it unread when his Dad's lawyer had given him the letter the first time.

For some reason staring at the white envelope now with his name written in his dad's handwriting, nudged him to finally read it.

Back then he didn't want to read anything from Mack Callahan. He'd still had unresolved anger at that time, towards his Dad.

However, since that day, so much had changed. There was some sixth sense inside him that told him it was time.

Maybe now he was finally ready to hear what his Dad had to say to him.

Denver slipped the wide leather strap off his shoulder and leaned the guitar against the bedroom wall.

Before he could change his mind, he hurried over to

the desk by the window and pulled the envelope out of its hiding place.

Seeing his name written on the front of the envelope in big black bold script, held him motionless.

Bold. Big. Brave.

Those words summed up how he remembered his Dad. But, now that he was older, he would add wise to that list.

He took a step back, his legs bumping into the side of the bed frame. Without thinking, he sunk down into its softness. His hand shook slightly as he opened the envelope and lifted the letter out of its hiding place.

Flattening out the creases in the thin, slightly yellowed paper, he started to read.

For my son, Denver. I think my letter to you, might be the toughest one I've written today.

I still remember the first day your mother and I saw you for the first time. You were just seven years old and living in a crumbling foster home with two other boys close to your age. When you looked up at the two of us with those big green eyes looking scared and with your arms trembling we just knew you were meant to be our own.

The trauma of losing your own birth mama weighed heavily on you, making you hesitant to come home with us, but in the end you did. Your mother and I were so happy when you joined our family.

It took months before the haunted look began to disappear from your eyes, but it did and you began to enjoy life at the ranch with your new family.

I know being part of our family and bearing the Callahan name hasn't always been easy on you.

I remember a time or two when you told me so.

Sorry for all the times we argued and didn't quite see eye to eye on certain things. I want you to know that even though we had some tough years, it only made my heart yearn to understand you better.

I know I made a lot of mistakes as your dad. I hope you can forgive me. I'm thankful we were able to talk through many of the problems we had.

Your mother and I were so excited to have you as our son. Our love for you has only grown since the first day we brought you home.

We've often thought of that first year when you and your six brothers joined our family. Each of you boys brought us so much joy and laughter.

You might not know it, but your six brothers admire you, each in their own way.

Your mother and I are proud of you too, son. I'm amazed that in spite of the tough beginning you had, you have been able to make your own way - build your own legacy - with your songs.

I'm sure your birth dad — if he knew about the man you've become — would be real proud of you, son. If you do see him again someday, please open your heart to forgive him.

As for your birth mom, I'm sure she's in heaven as pleased as punch with you. I'll have a tale or two to tell when I see her up there.

According to the Doc, that's going to be soon.

That's why I wanted to write you a letter, son.

I wanted to ask you to do something for me, sort of as a last request. Denver, I'm asking that despite the falling out you had with Sierra Baxter all those years ago, that you make things right. Do what you can to talk to her son.

I think she was really hurt when you left so suddenly before your wedding day. I haven't seen her much since that day. But, she's been heavy on my heart just the same.

It's important that you have a heart to heart conversation with her. Hurt like that has a way of festering inside us until it harms not only us, but everyone around us.

Now, it takes a little effort on your part to build enough trust so she'll listen to you, but do it. Offer your heartfelt apology, spend some time with her and take the time to really know her.

I'm asking that you take four weeks out of your busy concert schedule to come back to the ranch and make things right again.

I believe you could make a big difference in Sierra's life and in the lives of our family and our small town.

Who knows, maybe spending time with Sierra will bring the two of you together. It's possible that you might fall in love once again.

It would be your second chance at a happy life with the woman you loved years ago, much like I had with your mother. And a Christmas wedding would be the perfect way to end the year.

Your mother and I have always believed in the wonder of Christmas and the miracles that love can bring.

I know what I'm asking you to do is a difficult task, but I know you have a good heart. You're a fine man son and I'm proud of you.

Your scars have made you tough, but I believe inside you beats the heart of a compassionate and caring man.

If you agree to make things right with Sierra — and Mr.

MacCrae agrees that you have — then you will receive ten million dollars and a share (along with your six brothers) in the Callahan Manufacturing Company in Refuge Mountain.

The money from both should give you a good start on funding that dream you've been passionate to begin.

I wish I could be a fly on the wall to watch you get your second chance at love and live your dreams, but the Doc says that my time on this earth is short.

I'll be cheering you on from up above. Remember, I'm proud of you son. I love you, Dad.

A single tear trailed down Denver's cheek. With a shaky hand he wiped it away.

Mack Callahan always had a way of getting down to the heart of the matter.

He knew his adopted dad loved him. Reading through the letter again, he was touched by the fact that his dad had asked for his forgiveness.

Guilt clenched his belly into a fist.

It should have been the other way around. He should've asked for his dad's forgiveness.

Memories flashed through his thoughts of the times he had stubbornly been angry or shouted at his dad when he was a teenager.

His Dad had been firm but loving and kind with him. He didn't deserve the kindness, but it had been freely given anyway.

Mack Callahan had always told his sons of the importance of being honest and forgiving those who wronged you.

Which explained why his Dad asked him to make things right with Sierra.

But, to be required to spend four weeks with Sierra in order to receive his inheritance irked Denver.

He didn't like it that his Dad was managing his life even from the grave.

He admitted that he needed to apologize to Sierra, but he had planned on doing that this weekend. After that was done, he would promptly head back to his real life.

Denver threw the letter on the desk.

What was his dad thinking when he hatched this crazy plot to try to get him back together with Sierra?

He admitted it would be nice to receive his dad's inheritance money, but it wasn't like he needed it with the millions of sales he received from music albums, concerts and from other merchandise.

Shaking his head, he decided he wasn't going to think about that right now.

Slinging the shoulder straps of his guitar case over his shoulder, he headed out the door.

By the time he drove onto Deacon Miller's driveway, his shoulders were tense and his belly was tied in a tight knot.

He expelled a breath and set the basket down as he knocked on the door.

The large wood door swung wide open suddenly.

His mentor, a tall black man with wide shoulders and mostly grey head of hair, opened the door, a wide grin lighting up his face. "Aren't you a sight for sore eyes?"

Unexpectedly, those large arms wrapped around him in a tight embrace.

Warmth wrapped its way around Denver's heart and gave him the feeling of coming home.

He sighed, when he stepped back and looked into his mentor's kind eyes.

"Yeah. It's great to see you too, Deacon."

"Come on in." Deacon waved him inside and Denver picked up the basket and stepped inside his friend's large ranch house.

"Mom sent this over." He handed his friend the basket.

Deacon nodded and his eyes lit up as he grabbed the basket. "Tell your mom thank you very much. Mrs. Garrett makes tasty Thanksgiving turkey with all the trimmings."

"Deacon, I wanted to tell you sorry again for the loss of your Mary." They had briefly talked at the funeral. However, his friend had been surrounded by his own friends and folks from out of town that Denver hadn't wanted to intrude.

"Thank you my boy." Deacon released a long sigh, and his big brown eyes misted over. "She was the light of my life and not a day will go by where I won't miss her. But, she was exhausted these last few months."

The older man sighed heavily. "The doctor said her heart was simply tired when he gave her medication a few months back. But, I didn't realize she would be gone so soon." His friend wiped away a stray tear. "But, now she's finally at peace and I'm grateful for that."

Denver swallowed and nodded. His friend's grief was tangible and a wave of compassion filled him, but he didn't know what to say.

"But, I'm always glad when my friends stop by the house. It brings cheer to this ol' heart of mine." Deacon smiled gently and pulled a large pitcher of orange juice out of the fridge.

Pouring the juice into two tall glasses, Deacon handed one glass to him and walked to the large family room.

Denver sat on the single seat sofa. He liked this room, as around the room, was where his wife had placed many of Deacon's country music nominations and awards.

"Mary always went out of her way to show me she loved me. She did everything she knew to do, to encourage my dreams." Denver's gaze followed his friend's as he looked at the framed photos on the walls with famous country singers and pictures of him as a guest on many popular daytime talk shows.

"You were incredibly blessed to have a supportive wife, my friend. In fact, one of the first country songs I wrote for my first music album was inspired by yours and Mary's marriage."

Deacon's eyes grew wide and he slapped his hand to his knee. "Well son, let's hear it."

Pulling his guitar from the case, Denver sat down on the sofa, settling the guitar on one knee. His fingers strummed the familiar tune that fans everywhere loved.

You have always been my forever
You have always been my home.
Everywhere, every day in every way you are mine
I give you all of my love
Until the end of time.

LOOKING up as he strummed the last chord, Denver's heart warmed when he saw tears streaming down Deacon's cheeks.

He set the guitar up against the wall and handed his friend a box of tissues.

Even after Deacon wiped his eyes, tears still glistened like diamonds on his dark skin.

"I'm sorry, man." Denver didn't know what else to say. He was sad this song reminded Deacon of his loss.

He couldn't imagine the heartache his friend was going through with Mary's passing.

"I can't imagine the pain of loss you must be going through. You were married to the one woman you loved for a long time." Denver thought of all the women he dated, who he never thought of as possible life companions.

Most of them seemed to only want a relationship with him for what they could get from him. "That kind of committed love and support is very difficult to find nowadays."

"But it's not impossible to find, son." Deacon set down his empty glass, his gaze piercing his own. "I seem to remember you almost married a gal who loved you and really supported those dreams of yours."

Denver nodded and swallowed. "Yeah. Sierra was — and is — one of the good ones."

"Well, what are you waiting for? Go get her back. Marry the girl." Deacon had a no nonsense way of getting right to the point.

He squirmed slightly from his mentor's steady gaze as he realized the truth of his words.

"Well, there are three problems with that as far as I can see. The first is that I'm supposed to be back in Nashville in a couple of days as my music manager has planned another concert tour." Denver explained.

"Secondly, Sierra is still angry at me for leaving her on our wedding day years ago and doesn't seem to be interested in talking to me much. And the third problem is she's engaged to be married. I'm too late." Denver's throat ached with defeat. He felt an acute sense of loss.

Deacon sat up straight in his chair, his brown eyes full of strength and shining with a steadfast and firm resolve. "She is engaged, which is different than being married. You're not too late. Do you love her?"

Denver swallowed as the truth seemed forced out of him. "I do love her, but I really don't think I would make a good husband. I wouldn't be good for her."

"What are you saying? You can't play heartfelt songs like you just did about love, and then run away from it yourself!"

Denver realized he had always yearned for love and family, but had always been like an outsider looking in. He longed for something he thought he could never have.

His words faltered as he replied. "You know my story and how I grew up, Deacon. I've always been afraid of being like my dad and failing to be there for the people who needed me the most. You know what they say about bad blood and all that."

"Hogwash. If that were true, there wouldn't be people who grew up in foster homes, who end up marrying the women they love and making a happy home for their children." His friend leaned closer looking at him square on.

"You are not like your birth dad, Denver. Your birth mother was a saint and raised you well, God rest her soul." Deacon paused for a moment.

"But, I'm sure she would have been happy to know her son was adopted by Mack and Annie Callahan so they could finish what she started in raising you. Growing up in the Callahan household helped you learn about a loving father and how a large family helps and takes care of each other."

He shifted uneasily. "I know. And I'll always be grateful for their influence in my life. But, that doesn't change the fact that I don't think this is a good idea."

Deacon shook his head, a soft smile on his face. "No, son. What you are is afraid. You need to face it head on so you know what you're up against."

His mentor looked him in the eye. "I've never known you to stop yourself from going after something you want." Denver rubbed the back of his neck with one hand.

"You know me well. I've never been one to run away from a fight, especially when it's something -- or someone -- I want."

"Good. Now all you need to do is let your manager know that you'll be staying in your hometown a few weeks longer. Then make a plan as to how you're going to win back the woman you love." Deacon grinned looking quite pleased with himself.

Denver sighed and shook his head. "I'll think about what you've said. Maybe you're right."

"Maybe? You know I am." An expression of satisfaction showed in his mentor's eyes.

A half smile crossed Denver's face at his friend's confidence.

Even after he left Deacon's place and arrived back in his own room at the family ranch house, his friend's words continued to circle around and around in his head.

As usual, his mentor had been determined to dig down to the heart of what was holding him back.

Fear. Worry. Doubt.

All of those anxious thoughts were centered around the one person he wanted most. Sierra Baxter.

She was a constant reminder to him of all those things he longed for that he thought he could never have.

Family. Belonging. Love.

His mentor's words rang louder in his head. *What you are is afraid. You need to face it head on so you know what you're up against. I've never known you to run away from going after something you want.*

He'd never run away from a fight, yet. Choosing to win back Sierra was going to be the fight of his life.

The image of Sierra walking away from him with her fiancé by her side suddenly filled his thoughts.

There was no way he could let her go without a fight.

Taking the faded picture out of his wallet, he ran his fingers over their engagement photo once again. The watermarks had caused fading, but he could still see Sierra's beautiful smiling face.

This time he was going to do whatever it took to win her back.

She meant too much to him and he couldn't lose her again.

ierra

SIERRA POURED herself a cup of coffee.

Finally, a small break appeared in the large crowd of customers.

It wasn't usually this busy at *The Little Bean Cafe* on a Saturday, but there were a whole lot of new faces coming through their small town for Thanksgiving weekend.

The chatter of voices and clatter of cups from folks sitting in the cafe calmed her nerves.

Lately, she felt a little more on edge because her relationship with Stuart wasn't going as well as it had before.

Ever since Stu had shown his jealous side from when they talked with Denver at the baseball game, she had felt more unsettled about their relationship.

A couple days ago her fiancé had shown up at Grams and Granddad's farm for their Thanksgiving meal.

He'd been quite enthusiastic about eating Grams delicious turkey dinner with all the trimmings. Also, Stuart had tried to make an effort to get to know her son. It had encouraged her heart to see that.

Yet, she sensed this inner tension lately whenever they were together.

Well, they would need to talk again. Maybe after these next few weeks were over, they could sit down and have a serious talk.

Meanwhile, she had other things to think about. Important things, like her son.

Cody was asked by two boys his age — Caleb and Noah Flannery — if he could spend the afternoon and have a sleepover at his friend's house. After talking with their mom Casey, she agreed. It was good for Cody to have some new adventures with other boys his age.

Sierra had known Casey since high school, so she was confident her son was in good hands.

This was her son's first sleepover, so she was naturally a little concerned about how it would go.

Yet, she'd sent him off earlier today with a hug and a bright smile. It's what mom's did with their children, even when they were a little worried.

Sighing, she shoved all worries about Cody out of her mind and rubbing the back of her neck, tried to focus on her work.

She scrolled through the list of things she needed to get done at the coffee shop for the day.

Sierra was trying to get as many details taken care of ahead of time before the busy week that was coming up.

So far about half of the to do list had been checked off, so she only had half to go. There was so much to get organized.

Since she was the supervisor for her shift, she always had to organize each worker's schedules in advance. There were also all the products she needed to plan and order from their suppliers.

There was a lot to do, but she didn't mind.

Hopefully it wouldn't be long before she would own this coffee shop. She was eager to hear what the bank had to say about that.

That had always been one of her life goals. Sierra loved interacting with people and loved this small town and most of the people in it.

So, the idea of having a coffee shop where folks could come inside to find great food, encouraging conversation and a peaceful atmosphere was perfect.

"My dear, are you ready to host our town's Christmas Fair?" Her boss walked from the back storage room to the front counter her gaze landing on Sierra.

Mrs. Jenkins slipped on her coat and winked at her. An easy smile played at the corners of her mouth, her eyes sparkling with warmth.

Sierra paused to catch her breath. Fears of being in front of the camera were very real, and she was expected to begin on Monday.

"I think so." Sierra's hand shook slightly as she set the hot mug of coffee on the counter.

Lottie chuckled. "Feeling last minute nerves?"

"Yeah. A little." Sierra grimaced as a sense of uncertainty swept over her. "It's my first time as host, so maybe that's normal."

"It is. You'll do great, Sierra. You're really good at talking to people. And everyone around here already adores you." Her boss had a way of seeing the best in her that Sierra wished she saw in herself.

"Thanks, Mrs. Jenkins for believing in me as well as for being flexible with my work here so I can do this.

"You're welcome. This Christmas Fair benefits our whole community, so we will work around it."

"Thanks. Yes, I think it will benefit all folks from Refuge Mountain. I certainly intend to do my best as host."

Mrs. Jenkins slipped on a pair of soft finger gloves. "They should have thought of adding a co-host, to make things easier on you."

Sierra thought of Denver.

"Well, Mrs. Moore did ask Denver Callahan to co-host the Christmas Fair with me. He declined the offer as he has to get back to Nashville for a concert tour."

"Denver Callahan, huh?" Her boss's mouth twitched in amusement, her grey eyes gentle with teasing.

Heat began in her neck and crept up to her cheeks. "It's not like that. Yes, I was engaged to Denver, but that ended years ago. Besides, I'm engaged to Stuart now."

Mrs. Jenkins continued on as if she hadn't heard a thing she said. "Yes I know dear. But, Denver Callahan is a handsome young man with millions of country music fans. He would bring a lot of extra attention and new customers to our rural mountain town. It's too bad he said no."

Sierra knew Mrs. Jenkins was right about Denver's ability to draw a crowd. However, she would rather not have to be face to face with Denver for the next two weeks.

"I think it might be too difficult for us to work together." She was grateful he would be leaving after the holiday weekend.

Her boss adjusted her finger gloves before turning to her with a knowing glint in her grey eyes. "It might be difficult, but it might be just the thing to clear the air between the two of you."

Sierra grimaced, but recognized the truth of her words. Mrs. Jenkins knew, just like most of the local folks did, that Denver had left her just before they were to be married years ago. She realized her boss was just concerned for her.

Sierra shrugged, forcing a nonchalance about the whole thing that she didn't feel inside.

"As you say, he's leaving soon. Well, maybe it's for the best." She sighed. "I hope you have a good evening my dear. Call me, if you need me." Mrs. Jenkins waved and walked out the front door of the coffee shop onto the bustling main street.

Sierra watched her go, thinking about what she'd said about needing to clear the air between Denver and her. It was true, but it didn't make it easy.

Her belly tightened in knots knowing that she would need to talk to him.

Sierra began to scrub the counter, trying to vent her

frustration by cleaning. She often did that at Grams house growing up and her grandmother would tell her she didn't mind because the house could use a good cleaning.

She was just finishing up when the door opened again and entering the coffee shop alongside a blast of cool air was her friend Sarah. At her side was her grandfather, Angus MacDonald.

"Hello, Sarah. Hello, Mr. MacDonald. It's been a few months since I've seen you in town." Sierra walked around the counter and led them to their favorite table that had a clear view of the mountains on the other side of Refuge Mountain.

"Have you been keeping well?" Sierra asked as she quickly wiped the table.

Angus sat down and took off his hat, setting it on the table. "Aye. Except I can feel a cold winter coming in my bones."

"Granddad, your body always seems to know what the weather will be like before anyone else does." Sarah laughed lightly as she sat on the opposite bench across from her grandfather.

"Well, maybe it's true. Feels a little chilly today." Sierra replied with a smile. She could listen all day to these two and their lilting Scottish accents.

"I'll get you both a coffee and be back soon to take your order." She turned and after checking to see that other customers had what they needed, she hurried away.

Hurrying to make a fresh pot of coffee, she turned when she heard Sarah's voice behind her.

"I told Granddad I'd go get his coffee, but it's just an excuse to talk to you. Sierra, it's so good to have a woman to talk to. After I've been stuck in the cabin for so long, with only my Granddad and one or two of his friends that stop by to visit, I find myself longing for female company." Sarah smiled softly and pushed back her long, thick honey blond braid over her shoulder.

For a moment Sierra pictured her friend's life, as she lived alone with her Granddad on one of the mountains near their small town.

"I love to talk to you, Sarah. I wish we would see you more often." Sierra rinsed her cleaning cloth and set it by the sink and turned to look at her friend. "I think the last time I saw you was sometime in August."

"Yeah. Granddad only likes to make the trip away from the cabin and our animals once every three months for supplies. We've a couple of friends that don't mind looking after the animals for a few days. We might stay for the start of the Christmas Fair too."

Sierra smiled. "That would be fun for you both."

"Well, fun for me. Granddad doesn't like to spend much time in the village. It's too busy, he says." Sarah leaned closer, her violet blue eyes big and round. "I was at Lynda Goode's store, *A Goode Yarn* this morning getting the different color yarn I need for my newest crochet projects. Lynda told me they've asked you to host the Christmas Fair. Is that true?"

"Yes, it's true. And to tell you the truth, I'm a little nervous. But I'm hoping folks won't notice too much and they'll enjoy it anyway."

"Of course they'll enjoy it. You have a natural way of drawing people to you and what you're talking about,

Sierra. Plus, you'll look beautiful on television with your blue eyes and strawberry blonde hair."

"Ah, Sarah. You do know how to encourage me. Thank you."

"It's just the truth." Sarah smiled. "So any more news about when you're getting married?"

Sierra grinned. Her friend really was starved for conversation and news from folks in town.

"Sorry, no news there. We haven't set a wedding date yet. Stuart isn't happy about that, so we'll need to agree on one soon." Sierra sighed heavily. "And lately he's been more distrusting of me and that has been really frustrating."

"Why would you think that?" Sarah leaned her arms on the counter so their voices wouldn't be overheard.

A crease formed between Sierra's brows. "He made some comments after we saw Denver Callahan at the baseball game a few days ago."

Her friend nodded. "I'm sorry."

"After I informed Stu that Denver would be leaving after Thanksgiving weekend, he seemed to calm down."

"Sounds like he's jealous of your former fiancé." Sarah's violet eyes were fixed on hers.

"Yeah, I think so. Stu didn't like the way Denver was looking at me when we talked with him. But, I told him that was nonsense. He was just imagining things." Sierra shook her head. "Denver hasn't talked to me about anything of significance since he abandoned me on our wedding day years ago."

"But, maybe he regrets losing you. Maybe he still loves you."

Sierra's voice was resigned as she muttered. "Well, if he does, it's news to me."

Sarah leaned over with a small smile on her face and squeezed her hand. "Don't lose hope, Sierra. Somehow, everything will be made clear."

"I'm not so sure, but thank you for trying to encourage me." Sierra was used to her friend's encouraging words, but she didn't really believe them.

No, in fact as far as her relationship with men was concerned, everything was more confusing than ever.

She was happy when loud bubbling sounds erupted from the coffee maker and interrupted their chat. "Sounds like the coffee is ready."

Sierra poured hot coffee into two mugs and put the cream and sugar on a tray for her friend.

"Here you go."

Sarah breathed in the aroma and smiled. "Ah, this smells heavenly. Thank you Sierra for talking with me. I always feel better after I've had some girl talk with you."

Sierra grinned. "I'm glad. Now you bring the coffee to your Grandfather and I'll send someone soon with your food."

"Thanks." Sarah carried the steaming coffee mugs towards the table she shared with her grandfather.

Sierra had just asked her co-worker to double check on Sarah's food order, when the door opened again.

"Hi, Mom." Cody hurried inside and right behind him were Casey Flannery and her two boys.

Since Cody started his first year at the local elementary school, Sierra could no longer keep her son confined to the farm. All her son had known so far in his childhood was living on the farm with his mom, great-grandparents and uncle Eban.

Since he began school a few months ago, Cody had blossomed with new friendships. And Sierra was getting used to the fact that more of the folks from town were learning that she had a six year old son.

It was another reminder that she needed to speak with Denver before he heard about her son from the gossip mill in town.

Sierra's heart warmed at seeing her son. "Hi, pumpkin. This is a wonderful surprise." She crouched down to his eye level and kissed her son's cheeks, which were red from the chilly wind.

"Noah's mom said we could come in, so I could say goodnight to you." Cody squeezed her again before he was distracted by one of his friends Noah and Caleb.

"Thank you." Sierra smiled at Casey as she stood up. "Looks like the boys are having fun together."

Casey nodded. "A lot of fun. We went to Jeb and Sue Martin's animal farm. Your son was especially fond of the lamas."

Sierra smiled. "That's my Cody. He loves the animals…"

She was about to continue, when the door to the coffee shop swung open, and in walked Denver Callahan.

Her words came to an abrupt stop, her heart jumping in her chest.

A wave of both attraction and apprehension swept through her at the sight of him.

Her hand shook as she tucked a wisp of hair behind one ear.

Her eyes grew big and round as he stood by the door for the moment, assessing the place. For a moment she couldn't believe he was here in her coffee shop.

Denver soon spotted her and walked straight toward her. He didn't stop until his tall six foot frame towered over her.

Light smoldered in his green and gold-flecked eyes, only slightly shadowed by the black cowboy hat on his head.

He stared at her for a moment before he spoke. "Hi, Sierra. Thought I'd stop in and get a coffee."

"Sure. Let me get that for you quick and you can be on your way." Sierra hurried behind the counter and with shaky hands poured the hot black liquid into a to-go cup.

He followed her behind the counter.

"Don't hurry on my account. You can talk to your friends and I'll just wait here until you're done."

Sierra's heart accelerated. She looked up at him, and knew that look in his eyes. He really wanted to talk to her.

Problem was, she really wanted him to leave. Drops of hot coffee spilled on her hand as she poured it into the cup.

She winced and quickly set down the mug and put her hand under cool water.

As she dried her hands she looked over at her friend Casey with a forced smile and said, "You all go on and I'll see you tomorrow."

"Okay. All right boys, let's get going. We'll get a bite to eat and then we have some fun games to play later."

"Yay!" All three boys grinned at each other and zipped up their coat jackets.

"Mom, I just want to give you a goodnight hug." Without warning Cody came running around the counter to where Sierra stood next to Denver.

Sierra hunched down so she was eye level with her son, as his chubby arms went around her neck and he kissed her on the cheek.

"I love you, Mom."

"And I love you, little bean." She kissed his cheek and pulled up his coat zipper so it was all the way to the top.

"Mom? You have a son?" Denver's low voice behind her was velvet, yet edged with steel.

Slowly she stood to her feet, knowing that the moment of truth had finally arrived.

She raised her eyes to meet his.

His arms were crossed as he leaned against the counter. A throbbing pulse in his tense jaw line revealed his surprise and frustration.

Cool green eyes watched her like a hawk as he waited for her reply.

"Yes." Sierra's voice came out hoarse as if holding raw emotions in check.

All of a sudden, memories came back of being pregnant, alone and terrified.

Denver had missed all of it.

Regret filled her that she never told him about her son — *their* son.

SIERRA'S WORDS shook him to the core. He had a son.

Fear and anger knotted inside him. All these years he

had told women he dated that he didn't want to marry and that he didn't want children.

Yet, his son stood in front of him.

He shifted his gaze from Sierra to the little boy. The little guy must be what — all of five or six years old?

"How do you know my mom?" Cody's little boys voice pulled Denver out of the daze he was in.

"We grew up together in this small town."

He could tell the little guy was thinking about that.

A small smile turned up the corners of his mouth as saw Casey hurry around the counter toward his son. She held out her hand to him. "Cody, I think it's time we get going. It's getting late and you don't want to miss your chance to play those games right?"

Sierra sent her friend a shaky smile.

"Yay, I can't wait!" Easily distracted, his son turned to leave.

"Wait." Denver couldn't let him leave yet. He needed to know more. Walking towards the little boy, Denver sat on his haunches like he'd seen Sierra do as she talked to him.

He stared into green eyes that matched his own. Even his cheekbones were set high on his cheeks, much like what he saw when he looked in the mirror every morning.

His heart beat accelerated as the reality hit him. "What's your name?" He needed to know more.

"Cody."

"And how old are you?" Denver whispered, his voice shaky to his own ears.

"I turned six a few months ago." Cody held up five fingers on one chubby hand and a thumb with his other hand. "My mom says I'm tall for my age."

Denver could see that now. In fact, his birth mom had told him the same thing when he was that age.

It looked like the apple hadn't fallen far from the tree.

The little boy looked past his shoulder, over at his mom and smiled.

"Are you friends with my Mom?"

"Yeah. We've been friends for a long time."

"I didn't know. I'm glad." Cody smiled happily and turned to look at his friends. "I need to go, my friends are waiting for me. It was nice to meet you."

"It was nice to meet you too, buddy." Denver stood to his feet and watched as Cody gave his mom one last hug before he ran to catch up with his friends.

He watched them leave the coffee shop, before he turned to Sierra.

For a moment Denver saw a flash of something on her face that he'd never seen before.

Fear.

The expression passed over her features as quickly as a shadow before her features shuttered, closing off any further scrutiny.

"Looks like it's finally time for this conversation." Sierra expelled a shaky breath.

"Yeah." The knot in his belly only seemed to tighten.

"Let's go talk in the break room at the back."

She spoke to a co-worker quickly before she walked down a hallway toward the back of the building.

He followed her into a small room with a compact fridge, a microwave and three small tables encircled with chairs. Closing the door behind him, he stopped.

She turned and squared her shoulders as she swallowed.

Denver needed to know what would compel his former fiancé to withhold something from him that was so important.

"I want to know why you never told me I had a son?" He crossed his arms over his chest and a tick formed in his jaw as anger simmered just below the surface.

A crease formed between Sierra's brows and she grabbed the countertop near the small sink. It was almost as if she were steadying herself for this conversation.

"I'm sorry, Denver. I know it looks like I didn't make any effort to tell you about your son. But, I did try. Didn't you get the letter that I gave your mother?"

"What letter?"

"About three weeks after you didn't show up for our wedding day, I knew for sure that I was pregnant. You weren't answering any of my calls. So I texted you and told you I had something important to tell you. When you didn't respond, I wrote you a letter."

Denver ran one hand through his hair as memories washed over him. He deeply regretted that he had treated her so shabbily.

He had been so busy with his first set of concert tours that he hadn't been checking his phone very often.

"I do remember after a busy set of concert tours, finally my mom called me and said she mailed me a letter from you and that I should read it."

Sierra nodded. "Do you remember in the letter I wrote that there was something important I needed to tell you, but I wanted to talk to you face to face?"

"Yeah, I do remember you writing that." He stopped and inhaled a deep breath. "But, I also remember that Sid, my music manager, had packed my schedule so full that first year with concert tours that I had hardly any time to eat and sleep. In that letter, you were trying to tell me that you were pregnant?"

Sierra nodded, swallowing repeatedly. "Yes. That's what I was trying to tell you. And I was scared to write that letter too. Because I already knew how you felt about having children of your own."

He saw the tense lines on her face and the tight grip she had on the counter behind her.

A cold knot formed in his stomach as memories swept over him.

Before they got engaged he'd told Sierra he never wanted children. The image of his Dad walking out the door and his mother crying after him to ask him to stay would forever be imprinted in his mind.

However, none of those childhood memories were an excuse for how he'd treated Sierra.

"I know I didn't treat you right, Sierra. And I'm sorry. I truly regret all of the mistakes I made. I know that isn't enough. But, I plan to start making things right. And I want to start by getting to know my son."

"How are you going to do that? I thought you were leaving?" Sierra's words held an edge to them as if she expected him to do just that.

"I've changed my mind." He grinned as her eyes widened in disbelief. "In fact, I talked with Mrs. Moore this morning and told her if the co-host position was still available, I was available. So it looks like I'll be able to spend time with you again as well as my son."

Blue eyes wide and round stared at him across a sudden deafening silence.

"I don't know what to say."

"I know it's a surprise. But, I'm asking you to give me the time to spend with my son. It's time I got to know him. I want to make things right."

Uncertainty crept into her expression and almost undid him. He had a lot of past mistakes to make up for.

He only hoped someday Sierra could forgive him.

CHAPTER FIVE

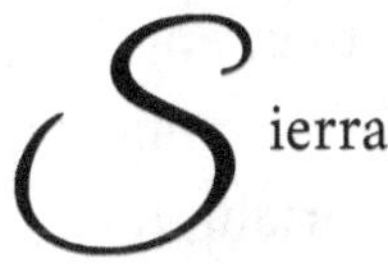ierra

Sierra arrived at the local television studio earlier than her scheduled time on Monday morning.

For the last two nights she had tossed and turned all night, thinking of the talk she had with Denver on Saturday night.

Now that he was aware of his son, Denver seemed committed to getting to know him.

That thought should have made her incredibly happy, and yet she was worried.

Experience had taught her to be wary. She'd been down this road before.

Years ago, Denver had also made another commitment to marry her, and ended up abandoning her instead.

How could she trust him this time with the one person who meant the world to her? Would he get to know his son and then leave the same way he left her?

Sighing heavily she opened one of the glass doors to the television station, her stomach in knots for the morning show ahead. She would spend the whole morning with Denver.

She prayed this day would pass by quickly.

Sierra wanted with all her heart for her son to be the one to choose if he wanted to get to know his dad.

She thought back to the walk she had with Cody on Sunday afternoon.

They went to the river and walked together, enjoying the nature around them. Now that Granddad could no longer take Cody, Sierra wanted the important family moments to continue.

She had talked to her son about his dad.

"I want to talk to you about your dad, Cody." Her belly had been in knots about how this conversation was going to go.

"Okay."

Sierra released a slow breath before continuing. "Your dad is in town and wants to spend some time getting to know you."

Her son's green eyes had widened and his mouth dropped open. "You told me he was long gone. That he wouldn't come back home."

She sensed Cody's disquiet and confusion. A sense of inadequacy as a mom swept over her. She never wanted to give her son a reason not to trust her.

Choosing her words carefully, she answered. "You're right. I did tell you that Cody because I honestly believed your Dad would never come back. But, now unexpectedly he's returned.

Do you want to see him and spend some time getting to know him?"

She was going to leave the decision up to her son. There was no way she was going to force him to get to know his dad.

"Yeah. When can I see him?" A strange, faintly eager look flashed in his eyes.

Sierra shook her head slowly, a slow smile spreading across her face. "You amaze me, kiddo."

She put one arm around his neck and with the other hand rubbed the top of his head before placing kisses on his head.

Tears pricked her eyes, threatening to spill over.

Her son was teaching her what it meant to let go of expectations from the past. Cody could just as easily have been mad at his dad, but instead he was eager to start new and fresh.

Cody giggled. "Mom, that's too many kisses."

Sierra chuckled. "Ah, you're starting to get too old now, I suppose."

"Maybe with the kisses. But, I'll always want a hug from you, Mom." He looked at her and shrugged.

"All right. As long as I can still get hugs from you, I'll be okay."

Her son looked at her. "So, when can I see my Dad? I've got a lot of stuff I want to show him and do with him. Does he have a dog?"

Sierra giggled. "You'll have to ask him about the dog, 'cause I don't know the answer to that question. But as to when you can meet him, I'll ask him to come to dinner tomorrow night. Would that be all right?"

"Goody! I'll need to tell my friend Noah, 'cause now I have a dad just like he does."

Sierra sighed heavily as she recalled the conversation with her son.

Ever since he had become friends with more boys his age that had fathers in their lives, Cody had told her a few times how sad he was that he didn't have a dad like they did.

Well, it looked like that was about to change.

Hanging up her light jacket, she walked into the filming room. Her hands shook slightly, a tell tale sign that she was nervous about being on camera co-hosting a television show for the first time.

She said hello to the two cameramen who were double checking the cameras.

"Miss Baxter?" A woman with a Spanish accent called her name and walked toward her. She looked to be in her thirties, with beautiful olive skin tones and a short styled look to her brown hair.

"Yes, that's me."

"I'm Sofia Hernandez. I'm the producer here at Refuge Mountain TV." Her big smile helped Sierra relax a little.

Sierra shook the offered hand in a firm grip. "It's nice to meet you, Ms. Hernandez."

"I understand you will be a co-host for our Christmas Fair." Sofia Hernandez smiled, looking down at the digital pad she held in her hand.

"Yes, along with Denver Callahan." Sierra looked around, but didn't see him.

"Yes. Mr. Callahan should be here soon. But since you're here, let's get you started. Let me introduce you to Ben and Will who are our camera men."

Sierra shook their hands.

"Now let me introduce you to Carla, our makeup artist. She'll be the person who will get you ready for the camera for the next two and a half weeks." Ms. Hernandez led her into another room where there were mirrors and chairs with all sorts of hair products and accessories.

Sierra smiled at a short buxom woman with glasses and black hair who appeared to be in her forties.

"Carla Jones, this is Sierra Baxter. She will need your artistic eye and touch ups for the camera today."

Carla eyed her up and down. "This girl? She's beautiful. The only touch ups she'll be needing is a concealing powder."

Heat rose to her cheeks and she smiled at the compliment.

"Well, you can get started then." I think our other co-host has arrived. Fifteen minutes before we begin."

"This won't take us long. Come sit here in front of the mirror and we'll begin." Carla patted a chair in front of a large mirror.

Sierra sat down and stared at herself in the mirror. Blue eyes stared back at her, anxious with slight shadows underneath.

Carla gently combed the brush through her wavy hair. "I love your long hair. I can see light reddish highlights mixed in with the golden blond colors."

"Grams says the hints of red in my hair are a warning to those that get to know me that along with my sunshiny goodness, also comes a wee bit of a temper."

Carla threw back her head and let out a peal of laughter. "Now, that's funny. I'll need to remember not to cross you."

Sierra grinned. "Don't worry. Most days I'm as gentle as a lamb."

Carla dabbed some makeup powder on her face and Sierra closed her eyes enjoying the pampering.

When the makeup artist was done, Sierra looked in the mirror, but instead of seeing herself, she saw Denver leaning a shoulder against the open door, a cowboy hat hung low on his head.

As their eyes met, she felt a shock run through her. His compelling and intense gaze riveted her to the spot.

If she didn't know better, she could almost believe he was still attracted to her. No, she told herself that was most certainly not true.

They had too many years and too many painful moments between them.

Her heart hammered against her ribs. She could sense the invisible web of attraction building between them.

She wrenched her gaze away from his. And gave herself a good talking to.

Sierra, this has to stop. You cannot allow yourself to be attracted to Denver. Don't forget you're engaged to Stuart and from past experience, Denver can't be trusted.

She expelled a quick breath.

Looking back at Carla, she saw her wide smile.

"Well, I do think the camera and the folks in our small town will simply love you." Carla declared as she turned Sierra in the chair to look at her closely. "Yep. You'll do. Now it's your co-host's turn."

"Thanks, Carla." Sierra smiled at the makeup artist and slipped out of the chair.

Grabbing her purse, she walked toward the door to where Denver stood.

"It's your turn." She spoke quickly hoping to hurry past him, but couldn't resist another glance at him.

His green eyes caught and held hers for a moment longer than necessary, his gaze as soft as a caress.

Every time his eyes met hers, her heart turned over in response.

This had to stop.

Words rushed out. "I'll see you in the studio." She did her best to make her voice sound cool and professional.

A sense of urgency and self-preservation drove her to hurry away from him.

When she arrived in the taping room, Ms. Hernandez directed her to where she was to sit. Two chairs were placed side by side behind a small white table.

Behind the chairs were windows on both sides of the back wall that looked out onto the steady stream of traffic on Main Street of Refuge Mountain.

Sierra took the notes for the day's taping and tried to focus on what they would be talking about.

Minutes later, Denver walked into the room and sat down on the chair beside her. She set her notes down on the table and turned to him.

"Ready to do this?"

"Yes." Sierra vowed to show him that she was unaffected by his presence.

"Did you get a chance to talk to our son?" Denver whispered his voice, hesitant and uneasy.

She turned and was surprised by the uncertainty in his

expression. "Yes, I did. And he says he would like to get to know you."

His mood seemed suddenly buoyant. "When?"

"Well, Grams said to ask if you wanted to come to the farm for dinner tomorrow night." Sierra held her breath, not sure what he would say to that. Her brother was not fond of Denver and Grams liked him, but still seemed unsure about him, ever since he didn't marry her years ago. Maybe a dinner together would be the start of mending things between them.

"I'll be there." Denver was about to say something else, but Ms. Hernandez interrupted.

"Okay, everyone. Remember, this will be recorded live. You're talking to all the friendly folks of Refuge Mountain and beyond. Have a good time and smile, everyone."

Sierra forced herself to smile and looked at the camera with the red light.

"You look beautiful in that red dress." Denver leaned forward, his voice low and compelling.

Her belly tingled with warmth at his compliment. Heat began in her neck and moved up to her cheeks. She wore the red dress because each day's show was focused on Christmas and she wanted her colors to match the holiday theme.

Sierra told herself she didn't wear this dress to please Denver.

Refusing to be distracted by him, she quickly turned to him and whispered. "Stop it. We're going live soon."

He grinned and winked at her.

Memories returned of when they were dating and he

always had some surprise or said something funny to make her smile. And it worked.

It seemed like he was up to his old tricks again.

Well, it wasn't going to work. Not this time.

"Going live in five, four, three, two…" Ms. Hernandez pointed at Sierra to begin.

"Good morning to all you fine folks of Refuge Mountain and beyond. Welcome to our annual Christmas Fair. As you know, each year we have a Christmas theme as a fun and interesting way to bring to you many of the interesting folks, places and businesses that are the bedrock of our small town." Sierra smiled.

"With me today to introduce this years' Christmas theme is a familiar face to all of you, my co-host Denver Callahan."

She turned to him and forced a bright smile.

Denver winked at her and turned toward the camera.

She was irritated with herself at how quickly he could break through the protective barrier she'd placed around herself.

Sierra released a slow breath to calm her irritation and tried to focus on what he was saying.

"Thank you, Sierra. It's an unexpected pleasure to be with you all. I was happy to learn that the theme for this year's Christmas Fair is the twelve days of Christmas."

"More than likely, many of you folks listening, have heard this familiar Christmas tune sung since you were a child. But in case you haven't, I thought I'd play this Christmas classic at the end of this morning's show to refresh your memory, so don't go away. Meanwhile, Sierra will give us a glimpse of the history behind the song."

"Thank you, Denver." Sierra warmed up to the topic, as she had always loved history. She began. "Some of my fondest memories I had growing up were singing the 12 Days of Christmas along with other catchy Christmas tunes as Grams and Granddad and my brother and I decorated the Christmas tree."

Smiling, she continued. "As it turns out, the history behind this Christmas song is interesting. During our research, we learned that the earliest printed version of this poem that researchers know of, dates back to seventeen hundred and eighty. This poem was found in a book titled *Mirth Without Mischief.* It was originally written as a chant or poem that wasn't set to music."

"We discovered that the twelve day celebration of Christmas was originally intended to start on Christmas Day and extend until the twelfth day known as the Feast of the Epiphany. It's also very likely that the origin of this original poem were written earlier than earlier and might very well have been French in origin."

"Another fun tidbit we learned was that it is highly probable that this poem began as a memory and forfeit game for twelfth night celebrations, which would have been spoken aloud and not sung."

"For instance, players would gather in a circle and the leader would recite a verse and each player would repeat it. Then the leader would add another verse, speak faster and it would keep going until a mistake was made by one of the players, who would drop out of the game. And of course, the last player standing was the winner."

Denver chuckled and added. "I wonder if it's a little like spin the bottle?" He turned to her and spoke again, his voice tender, almost a murmur. His gaze searched her eyes intently before dropping and lingering on her lips. "It's a kissing game and a favorite of mine."

Her heart jolted and her pulse pounded. Heat colored her cheeks under the intensity of his gaze.

Her hands shook slightly as she shuffled the notes in her hand. What was he doing going off script like that? Never mind his not-so-subtle hint that he had kissing on his mind.

Swallowing nervously, she turned to look back at the camera. After a pause, during which she fought for self-control, she continued. "It doesn't seem too similar to the game spin the bottle. Although, in my research, I discovered that if you can't remember a verse you owe your opponent a forfeit, which was usually a kiss or a piece of candy."

Sierra thought she heard a quiet chuckle from her co-host. She swallowed quickly refusing to look at him, determined to move away from the topic of kissing.

"However, during my research I learned that there was a Scottish holiday poem written that is also about the twelve days of Christmas. It's titled *The Yule Days* and is about a king sending his lady, partridges, geese, ducks, swans and more, just like the English poem."

The tune of this familiar carol as we sing it now, was composed by Frederic Austin back in the early twentieth century. It is based on the original poem, but both the lyrics and the melody were altered by the composer. So that's the history of this well loved Christmas tune. Next, we will learn a little more about the first day's gift from *True Love*."

Denver looked at her, his rogue grin firmly in place before he turned toward the camera. "To understand the meaning behind today's topic, we'll need to connect with our local reporter Ned Gentry. He's waiting for us over by the large Christmas tree in the center circle of Main Street."

Sierra saw Ned's face on the television screen that was beneath the cameras.

"Hey there, Ned." Denver touched the earpiece in his ear, to hear him better.

"Hello, Denver and Sierra."

Denver replied. "I see you are by the large Christmas tree that Refuge Mountain sets up annually at our town center. Do you have some more information about today's gift, A Partridge in a Pear Tree, for our viewers?"

"Yes, I do, Denver." Sierra watched on their live television monitor as the camera zoomed in to see a grey haired man wearing overalls and a red plaid winter jacket.

Ned spoke into the microphone with enthusiasm. "With me today is local farmer Jeb Martin, who owns Martin's family zoo outside of town. He knows a lot about this particular bird and has some ideas as to its meaning. Jeb, you have a few Partridges at your zoo. Would you share what you've learned about these particular birds?"

"I'd be glad to." Jeb Martin lifted his hat and scratched his head before continuing. "The partridge is a small bird that usually lives on the ground and I understand animal researchers group these birds in the same family along with pheasants, grouse and quail."

"At our zoo we have the Grey Partridge. These birds are shaped like chickens with plump bodies and small heads. They're not pets, but we keep them in a large enclosure with plenty of space to forage for food. Partridges are known to be a hardy bird, all of whom are willing to sacrifice themselves for their children."

Ned nodded. "Really? Sacrificing themselves for their children. Now that's true love, like the words in the Christmas classic. Back to you, Denver."

Denver hesitated for a moment and cleared his throat. "That kind of sacrifice brings a new level of commitment to true love's first gift."

"It does, doesn't it?" Sierra turned to Denver, her words full of meaning. Memories of how uncommitted he was years ago, filled her thoughts. Sacrifice hadn't seemed to be something he was interested in, not back then. But she wasn't going to go there.

Denver shifted in his chair beside her without saying a word.

She returned to her notes, needing to add some humor to the suddenly somber moment. "As a side note, there is a well known price index that calculates how much each of the twelve gifts listed in this Christmas song would cost."

"They've been creating this price index since nineteen hundred and eighty four. In today's dollars, for true love to buy all these gifts, it would cost around forty thousand dollars. That's pricey for all twelve Christmas gifts. Maybe the twelve Days of Christmas is much better given as a song than an actual physical gift."

Denver smiled and nodded.

"And speaking of songs, it looks like our time here is coming to a close. But, before we go, we promised all our listeners that Denver would sing this song to refresh our memories."

Denver stood to his feet and walked over the Christmas tree behind them. A chair had been placed on one side of the brightly lit tree and beside that a guitar was perched on a stand.

Sierra breathed in a deep breath and she turned to listen as Denver strummed the classic Christmas tune.

His low voice began singing the words to The Twelve Days of Christmas, making the song fun and entertaining for listeners.

His low sultry voice warmed her like it always had. Memories swiftly returned to the place and time they first met.

Denver was playing guitar and singing at Rusty's Café and Bar just off the main highway outside of their small town. It was the place his birth mom had worked as a waitress and bartender when he was a child. She had also played guitar and sang there.

She'd first seen him play there, when she worked as a waitress part-time during her last two years of High School.

He'd worn his used black cowboy hat on his head and form fitting jeans had hugged his muscular long legs.

As he sang, his gaze had singled her out from the crowd and it felt as if he was singing his latest love song just for her.

Sierra forced herself to stop thinking about days gone by. Their relationship had been over for years.

She looked at Denver only to see those hooded green eyes locking onto hers. As he sang the last line of the words — *my true love gave to me* — her belly burned with the dull ache of painful memories.

When he finally finished the song, Sierra breathed a heavy sigh of relief and turned back toward the cameras.

She didn't know how she was going to speak in normal tones, now that her emotions were all stirred up.

With shaky hands she picked up the notes on the table.

Clearing her throat, her voice came out raw and hoarse as her gaze met the camera. "Thank you, Denver for singing that Christmas song. It's a lovely reminder to us all of the importance of giving to others."

She continued speaking, setting down her notes. "Thank you, everyone for joining us today. Please, tune in again at the same time tomorrow, when we will share some interesting details about Day two's gift given by True Love — Two Turtledoves. We'll also be introducing a special guest. Goodbye, everyone."

Denver echoed. "Goodbye everyone and thanks for listening."

Sierra breathed a sigh of relief as they were finally off camera.

"Great show, everyone." Ms. Hernandez looked around the room with a wide smile lighting her face. "I believe this might be the best year yet for our town's Christmas Fair. I've been told we had a lot of viewers today. Let's see if we can get even more tomorrow. See you tomorrow everyone."

Sierra grabbed her notes, but as she stood to her feet, her foot slipped on the high heels she wore.

Falling sideways, she automatically reached out a hand

to steady herself on the table and unexpectedly grabbed an arm.

Two hands reached for her shoulders.

She looked up, captured by the faint light that twinkled in the depths of Denver's green eyes.

"Steady. I've got you." His hand slid down her arm and gently curled around her waist, pulling her close.

Warmth exploded from where his fingers touched her waist. Tingles spread throughout the length of her body at being held in this man's arms again.

Warning spasms of alarm erupted with her. What was she doing in her former fiancé's arms? She had to get away from his disturbing presence.

Quickly, she withdrew from his arms, trying to regain her balance.

"Thanks for your help. I guess I'm still getting used to the new shoes." Sierra glanced up at him, whispered, beginning to feel steady on her feet once more.

"I'm more than willing to catch you anytime you fall, Sierra." His mouth quirked with humor as he teased her.

To her annoyance, she found herself starting to blush.

Unexpectedly, another voice called out from the other side of the room.

"Sierra?" Stuart's heated tone came from near the main door of the studio. She flinched at hearing his voice and retreated back a little as his footsteps came closer.

"There you are, my dear." Stuart reached her side and kissed her cheek. "Hello, Denver."

"Stuart." Denver countered icily. He shot Stuart a cool look.

Stuart slipped his arm around her waist in a rare possessive move."Are you ready for our lunch date?"

Sierra nodded quickly, hoping to stop whatever fight seemed to be about to occur between Denver and Stuart.

Forcing a smile, she nodded. "Of course."

Glancing at Denver she saw his expression clouded in a flare of temper.

A sudden chill hung in the air.

"Thank you for your help today, Denver. I'll see you tomorrow." Sierra did her best to keep her voice neutral. With a quick nod, she turned towards Stuart.

Denver's warm voice whispered in her ear loud enough for Stuart to hear. "I look forward to seeing you tomorrow, beautiful."

Stuart grabbed her hand, his steps hurried as they left the building.

"Stu, not so fast, please. I can't run in these high heels. It makes my feet hurt." Sierra bit her lip and her eyes filled with tears of frustration.

Stuart slowed down and began ranting. "I can't stand Denver Callahan. He's constantly flirting with you, even though he knows very well that you're engaged to me."

"You should probably just ignore him. Don't let him get to you." Sierra expelled a weary sigh.

They went to the restaurant and sat at a corner table. "It didn't look like you were able to ignore Denver. When I walked into the studio just now, he had his arm around you. It looked like you were quite cozy."

Her blue eyes darkened like angry thunderclouds. "How do you know that I didn't trip and he was trying to hold me steady so I wouldn't fall?"

Stuart looked doubtful. "Is that what happened?"

"Yes, it was." She replied with a low voice, taut with anger. "However, today it seems that as far as you're concerned I'm guilty first before being proved innocent instead of the other way around."

Stuart sighed, running a hand through his hair. "You're right. I'm sorry, Sierra." After a few moments of chilly silence between them, he spoke again. "But you have to admit how I might have had that impression when I saw him holding you close."

His chiding tone caused bristles to crawl up her spine.

"Stuart, you aren't making things better between us by going on and on about it. I had hoped that you trusted me." Sierra did her best to hold her temper in check. She had only half finished her salad, when she put her fork down on her plate and set her napkin next to her plate.

"I do trust you, Sierra. I'm just weak when it comes to any man getting near you."

"I can't live like this — with you always finding fault or being jealous."

Stuart grumpily agreed. "I know. Sorry, Sierra."

They finished their meals, a cool truce between them.

As soon as her salad was finished, Sierra put her napkin beside her plate. "I'm sorry, Stuart. I need to go. It's almost time for my appointment at the bank."

"I'll call you later?" Stu's voice was hesitant. An uncertainty crept into his expression.

They walked toward Sierra's car. "Sure. I've got to go."

He waved as she drove away. Sierra sighed in relief, glad that their painful lunch together was over.

As she parked by the bank she wondered what she

was going to do about her relationship with Stuart. Ever since Denver arrived back in town, Stuart had been jealous.

Sierra's grip tightened on the steering wheel, her knuckles turning white. Something had to change and soon, because she couldn't listen day after day to Stuart's jealous remarks.

Only twenty minutes later she came out of the bank, tears falling down her cheeks. The lady at the bank rejected her loan application, saying she wasn't a good candidate to receive a business loan from their bank.

She was devastated. She had been counting on that loan.

Squaring her shoulders she got in her car, deciding that she would check with all the banks in the area.

She couldn't give up on her goal to own *The Little Bean Cafe.*

As she neared the Elementary school, her phone began to ring. She parked her car and answered the phone.

"Is that my beautiful niece's voice I hear?"

Sierra recognized the throaty low voice of her late mother's sister and sighed. "Hello, Aunt Serena. How are you?"

"I'm wonderful, especially today. Do you want to know why?" She lowered her voice, sounding purposefully mysterious.

A wave of apprehension coursed through Sierra. Aunt Serena sounded like she had another one of her surprises up her sleeves. From past experience, it wasn't something to look forward to.

"Sure."

"I've found a house here in Refuge Mountain. I'm here to stay."

Awkwardly, Sierra cleared her throat and stammered in bewilderment at the news. "In your letters you mentioned you wanted to come for a short visit."

"Well, I've changed my mind. I've decided to have a long visit with my late sister's daughter and son and of course my only grand nephew." Satisfaction filled her Aunt's tone of voice at the other end of the phone line.

"All right."

"And I would like to visit with you over coffee as soon as possible. Does tonight work?"

Sierra scrambled for an answer. "Sorry, I'm busy tonight. The next available time I have for coffee is tomorrow afternoon."

"All right then. I'll plan to meet you at the coffee shop at one o'clock sharp, okay?" Aunt Serena had a way of managing things to get her own way.

"Sure. Sounds good. I'll see you then." Sierra hung up the phone, and sighed heavily.

Aunt Serena arriving in town at a time when everything else seemed so jumbled in her life, wasn't very good timing. But she owed her mother's sister for taking her in when she had given birth to Cody six years ago.

So, she would meet her for coffee.

Hopefully, Aunt Serena wouldn't expect too much from her. Sometimes, her mother's sister asked too much of her, just because they were related by blood.

Her mind swirled, overwhelmed with all the difficult relationships she had to endure in the past week or so.

She would take one day at a time.

Tomorrow she would talk to Stuart again.

Maybe she could find a way to save their failing relationship. It's what she needed to do.

Or was her relationship with Stu a wall of protection against her attraction to Denver?

It didn't help that her former fiancé was doing his best to tease and flirt with her.

As much as she was still attracted to Denver, every fiber of her being warned her against him.

Somehow she was determined to place a bigger guard over her heart, so she wouldn't fall in love again with the same man who broke her heart.

CHAPTER SIX

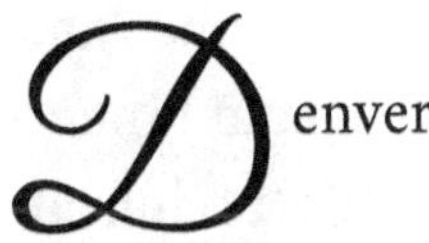enver

DENVER HURRIED up the stairs to the dining room, eager
for the day.

He was happy to be seeing Sierra again today.

Smiling to himself he hoped this would be the day he
would successfully break through the walls she put
around herself.

His mother and two brothers, Dakota and Hunter sat
together at the breakfast table drinking coffee.

He grabbed a muffin and poured himself a coffee from
the side table and sat next to his brother Dakota.

"So what's new with you lately, Denver?" Dakota's dark
brown eyes focused on him like a hawk. It was easy to
understand why the FBI had hired his brother to search
for missing persons for years. He had the instincts from

his mother's bloodline of the Lakota Native American tribe.

His brother could track people easily and he could also read them like a book.

"Actually, I finally received the blueprints for my house design. So this afternoon I am meeting with the General Contractor to look them over and set up a schedule for construction." Denver took a sip of hot coffee and saw surprised looks on the faces of his family members.

"You're going to build your house on the land from Dad?" Dakota raised one eyebrow as he studied him.

He chuckled. "Don't look so surprised. You must have known eventually I would do something with the land. And I believe I've found the perfect spot. The land I inherited borders the river and there's a stretch of hillside where the view includes the river, the mountains and much of the valley."

"Denver, that sounds like a beautiful location to build your house. I would love to see it." His mom took a sip of coffee her eyes big and round. "Sounds like a wonderful place for a family."

Denver sent her a half smile. "Yeah. I'll take you sometime Mom. But, first I need to get the house built. My goal is to get the project started next week."

"That soon?"

Dakota turned to his mom. "Denver here has the money and the connections. I'm sure they'll move their schedules around to accommodate his wishes."

Denver shrugged. "Maybe. I will admit I'm eager to get going on it."

"You're so much like your Dad, son." A soft smile lifted

the corners of his mom's mouth and her eyes had a faraway look to them. He could tell she was thinking back to when his Dad was still alive. "The moment he had an idea, your Dad didn't let the grass grow under his feet. He started it right away."

Denver smiled as he thought back to the one real cold winter they had in Montana and Dad had an idea for an ice skating rink.

The next day all his sons helped build the wood slats that surrounded the makeshift rink and within two days the water had frozen well enough that they were able to skate on it. Mack Callahan had definitely been a man of action.

"Thanks mom. That's high praise indeed."

Mrs. Garrett walked in and placed a new carafe of freshly brewed coffee on the table for everyone.

"None for me Mrs. Garrett as I've got to get going." Denver stood to his feet. "Thanks so much for another fine breakfast." He nodded at their family cook, always appreciating her delicious food.

He kissed his mom's cheek. "I won't be home until later in the evening as I'm going out for supper."

"All right. I will be listening to your live broadcast with Sierra today, Denver. Yesterday's live television event was wonderful." His mom squeezed his hand.

"Thanks mom. See you all later." He waved at his family and hurried outside.

As he drove down the highway toward Refuge Mountain, his thoughts returned to the beautiful blond who he would see soon.

His blood soared with unbidden memories of the way

Sierra responded to his teasing yesterday and to those few memorable moments when he'd held her in his arms.

Something intense had flared between them. She was even more beautiful now — on the outside and on the inside — than when they had dated years ago.

An undeniable magnetism was building between them and Denver wanted to do everything possible to ensure that continued.

However, her fiancé Stuart was definitely getting in the way of his plans to woo the mother of his son.

Was it too much to hope that Sierra would soon realize that Stuart was not the man she was supposed to spend her life with?

He was.

❧

SIERRA PARKED her car near the television station, noticing the storm clouds hovering in the sky above.

She hurried to get out of the car, hoping the rain clouds weren't a sign that a storm was brewing in other areas of her life.

Although, she had to admit lately as she thought about the constant arguments with Stuart, it sure felt like a storm.

She needed to talk to him and try to mend things between them.

Looking at her watch, Sierra realized she was thirty minutes early for the morning's live taping of the Christmas show.

Suddenly, she had the notion to visit Stuart's office to

say good morning and get their day started off on the right foot.

Hurrying down the sidewalk, she approached the Bittman and Witticombe accounting offices where Stuart worked.

She opened the door and saw that the secretary was busy on the phone, so she walked past her down the hallway.

Normally she had to wait until their office secretary sent him a phone message to announce her.

This time, it would be nice to surprise him.

Hopefully, he wouldn't mind being interrupted for a few minutes.

As she neared his office door, she heard the sound of papers shuffling and a low moan.

Was Stuart not feeling well?

Instead of knocking like she normally did, she opened his office door.

As she did, she stood there stunned. Her eyes widened and her jaw hung open at the sight in front of her.

Her fiancé's arms were wrapped around a woman, his mouth on her lips in a passionate kiss.

The blood began to pound in her temples and her face grew hot with humiliation and she swallowed the bile that rose to her throat.

Raw anger followed quickly on its heels.

"Hello Stuart." She didn't even recognize the chilly tone that erupted from her own lips. She forced herself to maintain an even tone, even though what she wanted to do was yell and throw things at him.

Stuart broke away from the woman in his arms. The

brunette stared at her for a moment, before shrugging her shoulders and looking back at Stuart.

"You should go Tammy." Stuart sighed heavily as the woman hurried out of the room.

Her throat seemed to close up and she glared at him with reproachful eyes. "I can't believe it. How could you Stuart?" She permitted herself a withering stare. "Just yesterday you were telling me how jealous you were that I worked closely with Denver, but today I come here to find you kissing another woman!" She was so furious she could hardly speak.

He stiffened as though she had struck him. "I'm sorry Sierra." He replied in a dull and troubled voice, his brown eyes avoiding her gaze.

She stood there shocked and shaken to her core.

She was too stunned to cry.

Shock caused words to wedge in her throat.

"Has this been going on the whole time we've been dating?" Suddenly she thought better of it. "Never mind. Don't answer that. It doesn't matter anymore."

Swiftly, she pulled the glove off of her left hand.

Tugging on her engagement ring, it slid off her ring finger easily.

As she dropped the ring on his office desk, the loud clunk disrupted the tense silence.

"Here's your engagement ring back. Suddenly, it's very clear to me that our relationship isn't going to work." She walked to the door and quickly turned around and faced him. Her pride had been seriously bruised by his behavior. A fresh wave of humiliation washed over her. "I hope she was worth it."

Tears of frustration and anger blinded her eyes, choking her voice. Before she could make a bigger fool of herself by crying, she rushed away.

Her clamped lips imprisoned a sob.

As she hurried out of the office building and down the sidewalk towards the television studio, her thoughts were jagged and painful.

How could Stuart do this to me? I thought he loved me and wanted to marry me?

Angrily she wiped tears from her eyes.

I'm not going to think about it right now. I have a show to co-host today. I'll have to think about it later. Right now I need to get going or I'm going to be late.

Forcing her legs to move, she hurried into the television studio and ran directly into a broad, well muscled chest.

Large strong hands gently clasped her shoulders, holding her close. For a moment, she welcomed the feeling of being cared for and tears made their way slowly down her cheeks.

She breathed in the scent of sandalwood and realized immediately she was held in Denver's arms.

An unwelcome blush crept into her cheeks and she stepped back.

His hands still gripped her shoulders, with one finger he lifted her chin, his gaze looking into her face probing and intense.

With his thumb he gently wiped away each stray tear. "Hey, what's this?"

The compassionate look in his green eyes, along with the concern in his voice, was nearly her undoing.

But she refused to allow herself to succumb to him. There was still too much pain and heartache from when he left her years ago.

She pulled away, fighting back the tears.

"I'll be okay." Swallowing back the emotion that threatened to clog her throat, she dared to glance up at him.

He hesitated, measuring her for a moment, and an uncertainty crept into his expression. He removed his hands from her shoulders and nodded.

Sierra looked at the time on her smartphone and noticed it was almost time for them to be on set in the Studio. She shifted on her feet. "I'd better go, or I'll be late."

"Sure. We'll talk later, Sierra." Denver's tone had a degree of warmth, but was also insistent.

Memories came back like a flash as to how determined he could actually be when he wanted something.

"Maybe. But right now, I've got to go." She boldly met his eyes and replied with an equal determination.

An easy smile played at the corners of his mouth, showing a confidence that was both frustrating and annoying.

Her back stiffened and she nodded quickly, before walking into the makeup artist's room to prepare for the show.

Somehow, she would make it through this morning's television show.

❧

DENVER WAS JUST FINISHING a conversation with Ms. Hernandez when Sierra entered the Studio.

Long strawberry blond hair hung in thick waves across one shoulder. Her bright blue eyes were highlighted by the royal blue sweater she wore. Sierra's beautiful oval face was set in the all too familiar mask of cool politeness.

Carla, their makeup artist, must have worked her magic because all traces of tears had disappeared from her eyes and cheeks. He couldn't be a hundred percent sure, but he strongly suspected Stuart had been the reason for those tears.

A fist tightened in his belly. Maybe he would need to have a chat with Stuart. There was no way he was going to let someone else bring her to tears. He'd already been responsible for far too many tears in Sierra's life and he didn't want anyone else adding to it.

Regret filled him. Soon they would need to have that much needed heart to heart talk.

He was determined to find out the answers to some of his questions when he went to Baxter's farm for dinner tonight.

He recalled the euphoria he felt when she had run straight into his arms. Those few moments had been like holding a little piece of heaven in his arms.

But just as quickly she'd moved away from him.

She didn't trust him.

Denver didn't blame her. Almost seven years ago now, he had broken her trust.

He sighed heavily.

There were a lot of mistakes he needed to make up for. It looked like he had his work cut out for him.

As she sat on the stool beside him, she grabbed her notes and read through them.

"One minute 'till showtime everyone." Ms. Hernandez spoke from where she stood across the room.

Sierra sat on the stool beside him, grabbing through her notes and reading through them.

Somehow they managed to get through the first part of the live show with no mishaps and an unspoken truce between them.

Denver introduced their reporter. "Today, we have Ned Gentry on location again with a local bird expert. Ned, we're all eager to hear more about these turtle doves. We are curious as to what could be the meaning behind True Love's gift for the second day of Christmas."

"Yes Denver, I wondered that myself." Ned's smiling face showed up on the live feed. "Luckily, you'll find out the answer to that question today. We're on location inside the bird sanctuary located a few miles south of Refuge Mountain. Here to answer our questions today is our local bird expert, Dr. Trisha Gray."

The camera zoomed out to show Ned standing beside a tall woman with dark rimmed glasses and black hair streaked with grey. There were wood walls and high ceilings that included many sunroofs dotted throughout. It was bright and sunny.

Ned turned to Dr. Gray and held the microphone in front of her lips. "It's my understanding you're an expert in many different species of birds. In your research, what can you tell us about turtle doves?"

"As you can see behind me, we have just over a dozen turtle doves in our sanctuary." Dr. Gray turned, pointing to a dozen white birds that perched on three different thick brown large ropes. The sturdy ropes stretched from one end to the other end of a tall enclosure giving the birds more room to move around.

"The Turtle Dove is smaller in build than other doves and it may be recognized by its browner color and the black and white striped patch on the side of its neck. The tail is wedge shaped with a dark centre and white borders and tips. It is a bird of open woodlands and most often eats mostly seeds like rapeseed, wheat, sesame, corn, millet safflower and sunflower seeds."

Ned asked. "What have you learned about the male and female birds?"

"For the Turtle Doves, courtship begins with the male making a lot of noise as it flies through the air and lands near the female. The male approaches the female with a puffed-out breast, bobbing head, and loud calls.

"The male then leads the female to potential nest sites, from which the female chooses one. It's interesting to note that the female dove builds the nest and the male flies about, gathering material to bring them to her. When the female lays her eggs, both male and female take turns to help incubate the eggs until they hatch."

Ned commented. "That is interesting. Are there any other details you can share about Turtle Doves that would help listeners understand why two of these birds would appear in this Christmas song?"

Dr. Gray continued to explain. "Yes, as a matter of fact I do. Since the song in question is a lively Christmas tune speaking of true love's gifts, it might help your listeners to be aware of the fact that male and female Turtle Doves mate with each other for life. Many people say two Turtle Doves symbolize love and faithfulness because they are monogamous and stay with each other for life, working together to build their nests, raising their young together."

Ned raised one eyebrow. "Turtle Doves mate for life and represent love and faithfulness. It finally makes sense why these birds are next to make an appearance in this Christmas song for True Love's gift."

The camera zoomed in on Ned's smiling face. "Back to you Denver and Sierra."

Sierra responded with a strain tone in her voice. "Yes it does." She glanced down quickly at her notes before looking up once again at the camera. "Love and Faithfulness are two virtues that our guest today has in spades."

She went on. "He's definitely a man who has not only seen success in his professional singing career, but also in his personal life as he was married to his wife Mary for over fifty years. He is someone whose life exemplifies love and faithfulness. Please welcome recording artist, Deacon Miller."

When Sierra finished speaking the camera zoomed to Deacon Miller who sat beside the Christmas tree, a guitar in hand.

As Sierra lifted her eyes, Denver caught a flash of pain that still flickered there. She dropped her lashes quickly to hide the hurt.

It shouldn't have surprised him that today's topic of the lifelong love and faithfulness of Turtle Doves, would re-open old wounds between them that had never been healed.

Pain squeezed his heart as memories assaulted his mind. Deep regret sliced through him and misery felt as heavy as a steel weight.

He really needed to have that talk with Sierra. It couldn't wait any longer.

She turned to listen to Deacon Miller share his story and introduce the song he was going to sing.

Shifting on his stool, Denver turned off all the other thoughts bombarding his mind and listened.

Deacon Miller began. "When I was asked by the good folks who organized this years Christmas Fair, to share my story and a love song, I realized the best place to start was to share about my Mary."

The older man's large brown eyes shimmered with tears as he spoke. "I met my Mary at a church barbecue over fifty years ago. Her family had just moved to town and after seeing her in church that first Sunday, I was determined to see her more often. Well, she didn't really take too well to me at first." Deacon chuckled and shook his head.

"In fact, after I finished my job at the tire shop for the day, she would hurry to walk on the other side of the street. Maybe she went the other way, because I was covered in oil and grease, I don't know. But I persisted."

Deacon smiled at the memory. "I would clean up after work and offer to carry her packages home from her work as a teacher. And often I would show up to talk to her at her parent's home. Finally after a year of being persistent and taking every chance I could get to woo Mary, she said yes to my marriage proposal."

A bittersweet smile lifted the corners of his mouth. "Marrying her was the best decision I ever made. In a way, we've been like the two Turtle Doves in that Christmas song. We've stuck together through good and bad times. For fifty-one years of marriage we've helped each other, we've built our family together and loved each other faithfully."

Deacon swallowed and a crease formed between his brows. "Now that the love of my life has gone on to her reward, I miss her more than words can say." He swallowed back emotion and paused for a moment, shifting the guitar on his knee before speaking. "A few years ago, I wrote a little country song for my Mary. I thought I'd sing it for you all today."

Denver shifted in his chair. His emotions had been touched as he'd listened to his friend Deacon's story about his wife.

They had truly loved each other.

What would it be like to have that kind of faithful love for one woman for over fifty years? To build a strong and loving foundation for their family?

A deep longing welled up inside of him for something he thought he could never have.

Deacon's song filled the studio.

You have always been the one. You have always been my own. You're my forever love. I'll love you until the end of time.

He wanted that — and he wanted it with Sierra.

Too bad he had allowed his fears to ruin his relationship with Sierra years ago.

Denver could honestly say when he had asked Sierra to be his wife the first time he had been too young to really understand what love and commitment really meant.

He had made a huge mistake in not marrying Sierra when he had the chance.

A picture formed in his mind and captivated his imagination. He saw himself walking hand in hand with Sierra. Cody was with them, playing with what looked to be a much younger sister. Everyone was smiling and happy.

He told himself that the picture he saw in his mind's eye couldn't possibly become reality.

He had too many strikes against him. First, Sierra was still angry with him for leaving years ago. Second, Sierra was already committed to marrying another man. Lastly, he had a big fear of being a father.

Even though he had every intention of doing his best by Cody, he was filled with overwhelming anxiety that he would be a failure as a father — just like his own dad had been.

Deep down, he believed he was his father's son with all his failures and mistakes -- and was convinced the apple didn't fall far from the tree.

A deep unaccustomed pain hit Denver's chest.

As Deacon strummed the last note of the song, Denver forced himself to smile and turned to face the camera. "Thank you Deacon for that amazing song and for reminding all of us of the importance of the gift of faithfulness and love."

He continued speaking, setting down his notes. "Thank you everyone for joining us today. Please, tune in again at the same time tomorrow, when we will share some interesting details about Day three's gift given by True Love — Three French Hens. Farmer Jeb Martin will be back to tell us more about the significance of these animals. Goodbye everyone."

Sierra echoed. "Goodbye everyone and thanks for watching."

Denver expelled a sigh of relief that they were finally off camera.

He turned to talk with Sierra, but she slipped off her stool. Her blond head was down and she looked like she was wiping away tears.

As he watched her hurry out of the studio, his first thought was to follow her to see what was wrong.

But, he had a feeling she wouldn't tell him what he wanted to know. Earlier, when she ran into him, Sierra had been crying. Somehow she had managed to avoid telling him what was the matter.

Tonight when he saw her for supper, he would need to find a way to get to the bottom of what was bothering her.

CHAPTER SEVEN

ierra

Tears blinded Sierra's eyes as she hurried out of the television studio.

As she walked down the sidewalk of Main Street, she dug inside her purse scrambling for a tissue.

Sierra dabbed the tissue at her eyes and cheeks, in an effort to get rid of all signs of tears.

Looking down at her watch, she realized that soon she was supposed to meet Aunt Serena at *The Little Bean Cafe* for lunch. She didn't want her aunt to see tears staining her face.

Her aunt had always been someone who asked a lot of questions, and she didn't need extra attention brought to the mess-ups in her life.

When she finished, Sierra tucked the tissue inside her

purse and forcing a smile on her face opened the door to the coffee shop.

Seeing her boss, Sierra walked to the counter to say a quick hello. "Hi Mrs. Jenkins. How's your day been?"

"Good and busy."

Sierra grinned. Her boss had often commented that it was good when they had a lot of traffic through the coffee shop. Sierra looked around, most of the tables were filled. Avery and two other waitresses were busy serving tables.

"I caught the live show for the Christmas Fair yesterday and today. It was really good. You're a natural on television, Sierra. Someday you should do more of that."

Sierra's cheeks heated. "Thanks for saying so, Mrs. Jenkins. But, I don't know if doing more live television shows is for me. I'm the quiet little mouse, remember?"

Mrs. Jenkins chuckled. "Well, as to that, I'll believe it when I see it. But, you and Denver do make a good team. I'm sure you two are drawing a whole lot of folks from our area and beyond to be part of the Christmas Fair."

"I hope the Christmas show is helping to expand the reach of our small town especially for the holidays. Mrs. Moore said that's what the town council was counting on." Sierra managed a hesitant smile.

Personally, she still wasn't convinced that co-hosting the television show with Denver was a good idea. His presence was far too disturbing to her peace of mind.

"There's a woman in the corner booth who says she's waiting for you." Sierra turned her head as Mrs. Jenkins spoke, nodding to the lady with black hair, who sat over by the corner window.

"Yes. That's my Aunt Serena." Sierra saw her aunt had noticed her and she nodded. "I'd better get going. Talk to you later, Mrs. Jenkins."

"Right you are, my dear."

Sierra navigated her way between the tables at the busy cafe and finally arrived at the corner booth.

"Aunt Serena, it's good to see you." Sierra slid onto the bench seat and looked across the table at her aunt.

Her aunt's cool gaze impaled her. "I was wondering if you were going to remember that I was waiting for you."

Sierra could tell by Aunt Serena's cool tone of voice that she disapproved of being kept waiting.

"Sorry for the delay, I just wanted to say hello to my boss." Sierra smiled at her aunt and sighed. "It's nice to see you again, Aunt."

Aunt Serena regarded her for a moment before offering a small smile. "Yes, it's good to see you too."

At that moment, they were interrupted by the waitress taking their order. Sierra talked a little with her friend Avery before she left to get their food.

Sierra turned her gaze back, only to find Aunt Serena watching her closely.

"You certainly seem to have a lot of friends."

Sierra smiled. "I do. I've been very blessed to live and work in a small town where most folks are very supportive and helpful to each other. If you decide to live here, you'll discover that for yourself."

"I'm pleased to tell you that I did find a house to lease. The realtor informed me it was old man Erickson's house. It's on old two story Victorian house on the corner of second street."

"I know that house. It's beautiful, much like the other lovely Victorian houses on that street. Mrs. Jenkins lives nearby and loves the area." Sierra said lightly. "I'm glad you found a place that suits you."

The waitress bought coffee and set their salads down in front of them. As they ate, they continued to talk.

"Yes. But now that I'm here, I want to have a chance to see you, Sierra and your son and hopefully your brother Eban. I feel I owe it to my sister to watch out for you." Her aunt studied her with a curious intensity.

"That's kind of you, Aunt." Her mom had passed away when Sierra was five years old, but Aunt Serena had always been faithful to write letters as she got older. Her aunt was her mom's stepsister, but had always referred to her mom as her sister in front of Sierra.

Aunt Serena gave her a slight nod in that queenly way of hers. "Good. Now then, tell me about your son."

Sierra grinned and dived into her favorite topic. "He's doing well. Cody has met new friends at school. He has joined a little league baseball team, and is loving it."

"That's good to hear. And how is your brother?" There was an edge to her aunt's voice.

Sierra grimaced. Her brother and aunt had never got along. Most likely it was because Eban had always been so protective of her and Aunt Serena liked to be the one in control.

"He's busier than ever taking care of the farm. Even more so, now that Granddad is unwell."

"I was sad to hear about that in your letter. Is your Granddad getting any better since his stroke?" Her aunt spoke with concern in her voice, reminding Sierra of her softer side.

"A little better. He talks a very little bit, but only Grams really understands him. Mostly he just points at something and we figure out what he wants. It's been hard on Grams, but Eban and Cody and I help out as much as we can."

'That's good. Your dad's side of the family has always been supportive and close. I believe that was one of the qualities that attracted my sister to your dad in the first place."

Sierra sighed as vague memories swirled around in her mind. "Grams told me as much as she could remember about mom and dad's relationship and marriage."

"I'm grateful that dad and mom valued having a close and supportive family. Someday I want that for myself." She swallowed back emotion as she thought about her recent broken relationship.

"Well you will. You wrote to me about your engagement to Stuart a few months ago, but I haven't heard much since. So, tell me when is the wedding date? Soon, I hope?" Aunt Serena's eyes widened and shone with excitement.

"About that." A heaviness centered in her chest and Sierra shook her head regretfully. "Sadly, I needed to break my engagement with Stuart."

"What? Why would you do a thing like that?" She heard her aunt's quick intake of breath and knew she'd surprised her.

"Well, I walked into his office today..." Sierra paused,

still feeling the pain from what she'd seen. "...and was shocked to find Stuart kissing another woman."

Sierra bit her lip until it throbbed like her pulse, refusing to cry.

"I'm sorry." Her aunt reached over and patted the top of her hand. "Don't worry, I'll talk to Stuart and see if we can get this resolved."

Startled hurt turned into frustration at her aunt's words. "No, you don't understand. He apologized for his actions already, but I gave Stuart back his engagement ring."

Sierra swallowed before continuing. "There's no way I can marry a man who would treat me so poorly. Grams has told me if the guy you're dating doesn't treat you well while you are dating, then you can expect the same or worse when you marry him. So, I've decided to take her advice."

Aunt Serena's mouth spread into a thin-lipped smile for a moment and the familiar mask of cool politeness descended. "I think you're making a big mistake not trying to fix your relationship. But, if that's the way you want it, I'll respect your decision."

"It is. Thanks for understanding." Sierra forced remote dignity into her voice as she looked over at her aunt.

"Well then, let's talk about something a little more cheery." Her aunt took a sip of her coffee and asked. "For instance, have you had any success getting a loan to buy the coffee shop?"

Nervously, Sierra bit her lip knowing her answer wouldn't meet her Aunt's expectations of her. "No, the bank turned down my loan application. I'm really disappointed, but I'll keep trying."

Aunt Serena smiled looking pleased with herself. "I have a wonderful idea. Forget about waiting for the banks to approve your loan application."

"What's your idea?" Sierra hesitated, her mind congested with doubts and fears.

"Well, how about if we bought this coffee shop together? I would lend you the money you need and be a silent partner, so to speak. You would run the everyday business and I would simply contribute money so you could own it now."

"That's a generous offer Aunt Serena. How would we work out the payments so I could pay back the loan?"

"Yes, you could pay back the loan in small monthly payments. We would be partners so all of the income would go into a joint business account. What do you think of that idea?" Her aunt's eyes brightened and her mood seemed suddenly buoyant.

Sierra shifted uneasily in her chair. "Let me think about it. And just so you know I'd only agree to this if I could pay my half of the down payment to buy the business."

Aunt Serena nodded. "I expected as much. Your mom was much the same way. I remember she was also a stickler for details and someone who always wanted to do her part to pay her own way."

Sierra smiled. "Well then, I guess I learned from the best."

"Yes, you did." Her aunt looked at her watch. "Well, I

need to get going. I promised the mover I would meet him at the house this afternoon."

Sierra nodded. "And I need to pick up Cody from school."

Aunt Serena paid for their lunch and together they walked outside. "I will call or text you in a couple days and we can talk more about making this coffee shop a partnership."

"Yes, let's do that." Sierra gave her aunt a quick hug and hurried to her car.

Sierra drove to her son's school, chewing her lower lip as she thought about Aunt Serena's offer to become her business partner. Her thoughts drifted between the pros and cons of the decision.

The truth was, she desperately needed help financially to be able to buy the coffee shop. Yet, the nagging in the back of her mind refused to be stilled.

Her aunt did like to be in control of anything that concerned her. Would Aunt Serena truly be a silent partner like she said?

Memories from years ago burned into her mind. Her brother had taken her to Aunt Serena's home to stay there to give birth to Cody.

Eban thought it best for her to be far away from some of the gossipy folks of Refuge Mountain.

Aunt Serena had watched her like a hawk, always wanting to know where she was and what she was doing throughout each day. Sierra shivered as she remembered.

However, maybe her aunt wouldn't be like that with the coffee shop.

At any rate, she had a few days to think about the offer.

At the moment, she was more concerned about the man who was coming to the farm for supper.

Denver Callahan was about to storm into her and her son's lives in a big way. Sierra wasn't sure she was ready for that.

Another round of painful memories resurfaced, reminding her not to let Denver get too close.

She couldn't allow herself to fall in love with him, only to be abandoned yet again.

Sierra sighed heavily, remembering the dark time she had gone through after he'd left her.

There was no way she could survive such a deep heartache again.

DENVER PARKED his truck beside Sierra's car and walked toward the front door of the ranch house.

He knocked and paced on the wide wooden porch, as nervous energy increased by the minute.

Since the start of this day his stomach had been churning with a mixture of anxiety and anticipation at how his supper visit tonight with the Baxter family would go.

Fear nipped at his heels that for some reason Sierra or his son wouldn't want to spend time with him.

Lord knew, he didn't deserve a second chance and he was grateful to receive one anyway.

He was so focused on his thoughts that he was caught off guard when the door opened. Sierra stood in front of him, a hesitant smile hovering over her lips.

Denver stood motionless for a moment, his gaze taking in her beauty. A warmth surged through him as he looked into her large blue eyes.

Strawberry blond hair framed her oval face and fell down to her narrow waist in waves that he remembered were as smooth as silk.

She wore a royal blue light sweater that highlighted her blue eyes and jeans that hugged her slender waist and legs.

As Denver's gaze traveled back to her face, his heart rate accelerated as he noticed the rush pink that stained her cheeks at his perusal. He was heartened as an awareness came over him that she wasn't as immune to him as she let him believe.

Sierra cleared her throat and bit her lip before she spoke. "Welcome Denver. Come on in. You're just in time for supper."

Stepping back she pushed the door wide open to give him a wide berth as he stepped inside the ranch house.

"I'll hang your coat and cowboy hat next to my brother's." She reached towards him and when Denver placed his hat onto her outstretched hand, their fingers touched and lingered for a moment.

Warm tingles went through his fingers and up his arm, spreading throughout his body.

For a moment she studied him with a curious intensity, her blue eyes darkening with emotion. The last time he'd seen Sierra, she'd been crying. He was thankful she seemed okay now.

Denver wanted to ask her what happened, but that would have to wait until later.

He stepped closer and with one hand softly brushed the back of his fingers to the rose petal softness of her cheek.

"Denver, is that you at the door?" Sierra's Grandmother's silvery voice could be heard from the kitchen.

Startled, Sierra jerked away from his touch. Her fingers gripped his cowboy hat and she swivelled quickly to place his hat beside Eban's. He slipped his jacket off his shoulders and Sierra grabbed it quickly and hung it in place.

Sierra turned to him, pink staining her cheeks.

He turned up his smile a notch hoping it would help Sierra relax. "Yes, Mrs. Baxter, I'm here. And supper smells delicious."

He followed Sierra up the few stairs that led to the large open room where he could see the kitchen, dining room and large family room all at once.

Sierra's grandmother walked toward him, a smile on her wrinkled face. "Denver, it's good to see you again. We've heard your voice on the radio, but it's much better seeing you in person."

Denver met the smile and the hand, which was offered. "It's good to see you too. Thanks for inviting me over."

"Well, you're just in time because the food is ready."

"It smells heavenly, Mrs. Baxter."

"I'm glad. And please do call me Grams just like everyone else." Her smile was contagious and he smiled easily. "Sierra will show you to the table, while I call the others."

"Grams needs to sit beside Granddad to cut his food and help him eat." Sierra explained as she led him to the large dining room table. "So it's probably best if you sit at the other end of the table with Cody next to you."

"Sounds good."

It wasn't long before the others joined them. Sierra sat Cody in the middle of them both. Grams pushed her husband's wheelchair to the end of the table. Eban sat on the other side of the table, a furrow between his brows.

Grams looked at her grandson and spoke. "Eban you remember Denver Callahan, of course."

Eban reluctantly nodded in his direction. "Hello, Denver."

Denver chose to ignore the obvious disapproval Sierra's brother had of him. He understood Sierra's brother's reluctance to accept him back into their family's life. He hoped with time he could win him over. "It's good to see you again, Eban."

Sierra's brother gave him a quick nod and turned to look at his grandmother.

Denver looked across the table at Sierra's Granddad and couldn't make out his slurred words.

"Since my husband's stroke, sometimes it's been difficult for us to understand his words. But, I believe he's trying to say, 'Welcome home Denver.'"

A war of emotions raged within him, and tears pricked the back of his eyes. Other than his own mom and brothers, no one had actually said those words.

It made him want to be a better man. It made him want to become a man that Sierra, his son and her whole family could be proud of. Rapidly he blinked, doing his best not to allow messy emotions to spill over.

"That means a lot to hear you say that. Thank you Mr. Baxter." Denver sent him a thoughtful smile.

The older man's chin quivered slightly as he tried to form a smile.

Grams turned to her husband, lightly grasped his hand and squeezed it gently. "Well, this is a lovely way to begin our meal." She smiled at everyone seated around the table. "I'll say grace and then we'll eat." Grams said a quick prayer of thanksgiving for the food.

The roast beef, mashed potatoes and gravy were so delicious that there was silence for the first part of the meal.

As soon as Cody finished his food, he turned to him. "My mom told me you're my dad. Does that mean we can do stuff together like my friends do with their dads?"

"Yeah. I'd like that."

"Me too. Can I show you to my room? I want you to see my pet hamster and cat."

Denver grinned and winked at Sierra. "If your mom and Grams say it's all right."

"Mom, can I take Denver to show him my animals?" Cody's eyes lit up.

"Of course you can, little bean." Sierra leaned over and quickly kissed her son on the forehead.

"Goody." Cody stood up from his chair and turned to Denver. "Come on, I'll show you."

Cody grabbed his hand and pulled him down the hallway and into a large bedroom. There was a single bed against one wall and cartoon characters were sprinkled over the blanket that lay on top.

It was definitely a boys room with a baseball glove and

bat in the corner and some dirty clothes thrown in one corner.

His son led him over to the other corner near the window where a cage sat on top of a small table.

Cody pointed to a furry creature in the cage. "This is my pet hamster."

"Ah. Looks like he's busy running." The hamster was inside the wheel, his little paws moving quickly, causing it to turn. "What's his name?"

"His name is Jumper. And I'm responsible to feed him everyday."

Denver smiled, looking closely at the brown fur ball in the cage. "That's an important job to remember to feed your hamster everyday. But I'm sure you do a good job of it."

Cody's shoulders straightened a little more as Denver turned back to look at him. "Thanks."

At the sound of a meow they both turned to see a long haired brown and orange cat jumped on the bed. Cody walked over to the bed and sat down and picked up the cat. "I also have to remember to feed my cat everyday too. Sometimes she sleeps with me."

"How nice to have a pet that keeps you warm at night." Denver grinned and ran one hand over the soft fur. "What's your cat's name?"

"Patches. Because she looks like her fur is made up of patches." Cody snuggled Patches and kissed the top of her fuzzy head. "Do you like animals Denver?"

"I do."

"I'm glad." Cody looked over at him, his green eyes wide and bright. "Do you want to hold Patches?"

Denver nodded. "I'd be happy to." He snuggled his son's cat in his arms and slowly petted her soft fur.

"I'm glad you like animals too. When I grow up I'm going to have horses and dogs and everything. Do you have a dog?"

"I don't, but my mom does on the ranch. In fact, our dogs — Jack and Jill — just had a litter of puppies only six weeks ago. I'll have to take you to the ranch soon, so you can see them."

"I'd like that. Do you play baseball too? Maybe we could play catch together. Uncle Eban plays with me sometimes, but he usually has to work on the farm." A sad smile formed on his son's mouth.

"Well, I'll need to play catch with you soon. I'd be happy to help you learn to play ball."

"This is going to be so much fun. I'm glad you came back, Denver. Are you going to stay so we can do stuff together?" Cody looked at him, his heart in his eyes.

"You would like that?" Denver hadn't really thought about what it would mean to have a son. But he wanted to spend time with Cody and really get to know him. He had a lot of missed moments to make up for.

"I would like to spend time with you, more than anything in the world."

Hearing his son's words, Denver felt like his heart was doing cartwheels in his chest.

"Then we'll make that happen." Denver leaned a shoulder against his son's smaller frame and looked into his son's hopeful face. "I would love to spend time with you, Cody."

It felt so good to have a son.

Determination rose up on the inside. He would do everything in his power to be a good father. Doubts and fears nagged at him, causing questions to roll around in his thoughts.

Would he be able to be the kind of dad Cody needed, or would he fail at this just like his birth dad failed him and his mom?

He couldn't let that happen.

Denver would do everything possible to see to it that he wouldn't fail his son.

"I've got to get going, but I want to say thanks again for the delicious supper, Grams."

Sierra watched her grandmother's pleased expression at Denver's words.

"Don't be a stranger, Denver. I expect to see you back here soon."

"Yes, ma'am."

A small smile lifted the corners of her mouth as Sierra followed Denver to the front door.

He quickly reached for his cowboy hat and light jacket.

"Come with me outside for a moment." Denver whispered.

She nodded quickly and grabbed her light sweater that hung on the coat rack.

Denver held the door open and she walked past him out onto the large deck that surrounded the old ranch house.

At the far end of the deck was a wooden bench seat swing built for two.

"Let's sit down for a minute so we can talk." Denver grabbed her hand and led her to the wooden bench swing.

Tingles spread from her fingers and up her arm from the touch of his hand.

She sat down on the wooden swing, making sure there was space between them before she looked up.

His nearness made her senses spin and she did her best to squelch the excitement his nearness always had on her.

Denver turned, his gaze traveling over her face, searching her eyes.

She noticed he was watching her intently and was desperate to talk to switch his attention to something else.

"Did you enjoy Gram's food?" The hurried words out of her mouth, caused him to grin.

He'd always known when she was nervous she began to chatter.

"I did. But your grandmother has always been a great cook."

"True." Sierra had to agree. "And your chat with Cody, did that go okay?"

"Better than okay. He's a son to be proud of and I know that's because you're a great mom."

Tears pricked her eyes at his words. "Thank you for saying that, it means a lot."

"Just calling it how I see it." Denver reached over and squeezed her hand that lay on her lap. "I'm truly sorry, I haven't been there for you all these years to help raise our son. I promise to do better from here on out."

Sierra swallowed quickly. "I hope you mean that. Cody

would be terribly hurt if he grew to love you and then you had to leave."

Unspoken memories of Denver leaving her, filled the night air with tension.

Denver sighed heavily. "I know. And I promise to do right by him and you, Sierra."

Despite his whispered words, doubt and fear plagued her as she remembered how he suddenly left her years ago. But, she knew she needed to give him a chance with Cody.

"Okay. I'm glad."

Denver was quiet for a moment. "I was thinking of taking Cody on Saturday to the ranch. That way he could get to know his grandmother and uncles from my family."

She nodded with a small smile, but her belly tightened in pain that Cody had never met his father's side of the family. "That's a good idea."

Sierra hesitated, but knew she needed to tell him what happened in the past six years. "I'm sorry that I didn't let your mom or your dad know that Cody was your son, Denver. In fact, I went away from our small town, to my Aunt Serena's home to give birth to Cody. I didn't want all sorts of gossip to spread about me. That's also the reason I've continued living on Grams and Granddad's farm."

"It's okay, Sierra. I understand why you felt you needed to keep the details of our son's birth quiet." Sierra could see the conflicting emotions on Denver's face. "That's all in the past. All we have a chance right now to begin again and make a better future for our son."

"I agree. And I think he would love to meet your family." Sierra tried to turn their conversation to a lighter note.

"And don't forget about all those animals your family has on the ranch. Cody will be thrilled."

Denver grinned.

Sierra giggled. "First it was the hamster, then it was the cat and now he's asking for a dog of his own. Did he tell you that Patches the cat sleeps with him at night?"

"Yeah. Our son sure loves his pet animals. He'll certainly see a few thousand cattle and other animals at the Callahan ranch. I'm looking forward to taking him on Saturday." Denver turned to her a question in his eyes. "You should come with us."

The idea sent her spirits soaring, but she knew she should refuse. "I can't. Besides, this should be your time with Cody."

"It will be my time with Cody even if you're with us. And what do you mean, you can't? Is Stuart being obnoxious again?"

Her smile disappeared as she thought of Stuart. Moisture filled her eyes and she whispered softly. "No, Stuart isn't holding me back. At least not any more."

"What do you mean? If he hurts you, I'll go have that chat with him I've been planning on."

Sierra chuckled. "Thanks for wanting to protect me, Denver. But, it's not necessary. I ended my engagement to Stuart this morning, so you see there's no need to have that chat."

"So, that's why you were crying this morning at the television studio." She nodded and swallowed embarrassed that he'd seen her tears. Denver slipped his arm around her shoulders, pulling her into his embrace.

"I would ask what happened, but it's none of my business, so long as you're okay. Everything is going to be all right. He wasn't good enough for you anyway."

She smiled at his words and wiped the tears that made a trail down her cheeks.

His hand traced tiny circles on her arm and her skin tingled from the contact. She felt him kiss the top of her head and she felt so protected and comforted in his arms.

For some reason, his tenderness caused more tears to stream down her cheeks.

He cupped her chin, lifting it so she was compelled to meet his gaze. With his thumb, he gently removed the tears from her cheeks and then his lips followed.

The touch of his lips was gentle on her eyelids, her nose and her cheeks until his lips covered hers with a warm sweetness.

It was a kiss for her tired soul to melt into, even though her mind tried to tell her to resist.

With his one hand he explored the hollows of her back, while his other traced caresses along her neck and cheek. She relaxed, sinking into his cushioning embrace.

She kissed him back enjoying being in his embrace until suddenly he raised his mouth from hers.

Denver whispered softly, his eyes warm and tender. "I've missed holding you in my arms, Sierra."

Sierra stared motionless into green eyes that seemed to caress her very soul.

She was shocked by her own eager response to his kisses.

Fear gripped her emotions and she pulled away quickly from his embrace.

Standing to her feet she whispered in the cool night air. "I can't do this again, Denver. I just can't."

Turning swiftly, she ran across the deck and opened the door to the house, closing it softly behind her.

Leaning her head against the solid wood of the door, she let the tears flow down her cheeks.

She couldn't let her attraction to Denver cloud what she knew to be true. He wasn't a man who could truly commit to the woman he loved. He'd already proven that seven years ago and she had no reason to believe that anything had changed.

Crossing her arms over her chest, she wept for all that she'd lost and would never get back again.

CHAPTER EIGHT

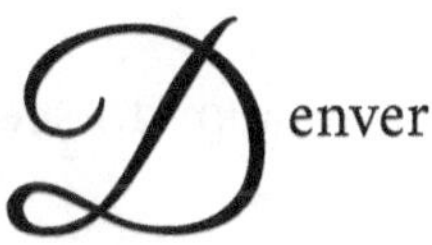enver

"I'M LOOKING FORWARD to seeing your two big dogs and the puppies on your ranch." Cody sat in the middle seat of his truck, between him and Sierra.

His small face was lit up with excitement.

Denver had just picked the two of them up from Baxter's farm.

He had been a little worried, ever since Sierra had run away from him that night he'd come to the farm for supper.

Every time he'd seen her at the television studio since that day, he'd done his best to be extra kind and considerate of her.

Denver couldn't resist helping Sierra slip on her jacket or accidentally touching her hand.

He wanted her to trust him. He wanted her to respect him. He wanted her to fall in love with him again.

But, now he realized he needed to build trust with her once more. He really hoped today would help to break down the walls around her heavily guarded heart.

He hoped she would let him in.

He looked over at her and his heart jolted and pulse pounded. He knew she was by no means blind to his attraction.

So far she kept putting him off, but he was determined to break down her walls and win her trust and her love.

Sierra offered him a small, hesitant smile before looking down at her son.

His gaze followed hers, looking at Cody, happy to see the excitement on his son's upturned face.

"Good. I think they'll love you, Cody." Denver grinned as he turned off the highway and onto the dirt road that led them towards the Triple C Ranch.

His son's eyebrows lifted in surprise. "Oh man, I can't wait. What are their names again? I forgot."

"Jack and Jill are the two big dogs. They are Bernese Mountain dogs with brown, black and white coloring. They're big, strong and affectionate dogs who are always doing their best to compete for your affection. They love to be included in all family activities. The puppies don't have names yet. I think they will love you, Cody."

"Mom, did you hear that? Two big dogs and tiny puppies that I can play with." Cody turned to Sierra who sat on the passenger seat.

"I did, little bean. Sounds like this is going to be a

perfect day for you." Sierra squeezed her son's hand and looked over at Denver.

Denver grinned and nodded. "It's going to be a perfect day for all of us."

Uncertainty crept into Sierra's expression as he glanced her way. He promised himself that he would do everything possible to erase any lingering doubts and uncertainty his former fiancé had of him.

Today would be a good day to begin.

He drove onto the large yard of the Callahan Ranch and parked his truck near the barn.

Opening the truck door, he heard loud barks and saw dust flying up in the air as the two dogs ran to greet them.

Cody hopped out of the truck on his side, his green eyes wide with delight as the large dogs ran straight to him.

"The big dog is Jack and the smaller one is Jill." Denver crouched down on his haunches so he could look Cody in the eye, and hopefully dispel any fears.

"Don't worry they won't bite. These are very friendly dogs." Almost as if they needed to prove it, Jack licked Cody's hand and Jill bumped against him.

Denver patted Jill's thick fur. "See, Jill is bumping against you. It's her way of asking if you would pet her."

"Really? Dogs know how to ask for things too?" A probing curiosity came into his son's green eyes.

"You bet. Animals know how to ask you for those things they want." Denver watched as a new under-standing came over Cody's features.

His son reached up and began to run his fingers

through both Jack and Jill's fur. Both dogs continued to get close to him, loving the attention.

Denver stood to his feet and saw Sierra watching him, with blue eyes that were filled with a curious deep longing.

He walked over to where she stood.

Her whispered words were heartfelt. "You're patient with Cody when you teach him new things. Thanks for that."

"You're welcome. I'm a big believer that children should grow up with as few emotional scars as possible." His faint smile held a touch of sadness.

"I agree. You surprise me in a good way sometimes." Sierra eyed him with a questioning expression as if she was trying to figure him out.

He chuckled. "You can expect more of those moments today." Reaching an arm lightly around her shoulders, he pulled her close for a moment.

"Come on, buddy. Let's go see if everybody is ready to go sledding." Denver kept his arm around Sierra and held Cody's hand as they walked toward the house.

A sense of contentment and peace filled him. The day had just begun and already it felt perfect, simply because he had his family by his side.

As they neared the Callahan family's large ranch house, Sierra's shoulders tingled with warmth from Denver's embrace.

She could admit to enjoying the very special attention

Denver had been giving her ever since he had come to the farm for supper a few days ago.

Ever since she'd hurried away from him that night after he kissed her, she had been convinced he would stop speaking to her or back away completely.

But, he'd done the opposite of what she'd expected. He'd shown her kindness and had been considerate of her feelings.

Was she mistaken about Denver?

Just now, he'd surprised her with how patient he was with her son. With their son. This was the same man who had told her emphatically he never wanted children. Yet, today he was showing the patience and gentleness of a family man.

For so many years — ever since Denver had deserted her on their wedding day — she'd been angry with him. She had kept walls around her heart. Stuart's recent betrayal of her trust seemed to justify the reason she'd placed unbreakable walls around her heart in the first place.

But, Denver's recent tender words and actions since he arrived home confused her. And she found that she had to conquer her involuntary reactions to that gentle loving look of his.

Fear filled her senses because lately instead of wanting to run away from him, she experienced a weird urge to walk straight into his arms.

She couldn't let that happen.

Sierra fought to control her swirling emotions as she saw the Callahan family walk out the door and toward them.

She grabbed Cody's hand. This would be the first time Denver's family met her son. Would they accept him?

"Denver, you arrived just in time or we were going to start sledding without you." Denver's mom walked toward followed quickly by his six brothers including Wyatt and his wife Abby and their two adopted boys. They were all dressed in her warm winter clothes ready to have fun in the snow.

Denver kissed his mom's cheek and then he turned to Sierra and Cody. "Mom, you remember Sierra. And this is your new grandson that I've been telling you about." Sierra's eyes grew wide and she looked at Denver. She was grateful he had told his mom about Cody, it would make today a little easier for everyone.

Mrs. Callahan kissed Sierra's cheek. "Sierra, I'm happy you're here." His mom's kind smile melted her fears. Denver's mom then looked at her son. "And you must be my grandson Cody. Welcome to the family, young man."

"Can I call you Grandma?" Cody seemed to be taking being introduced to his dad's side of the family in stride. Sierra was amazed that her son was so easygoing.

"Of course you can. Why don't you come with me. Do you like sledding?" Cody reached for his new grandma's hand and began to walk with her.

Denver grabbed her hand and they followed everyone. She turned to him and whispered. "Thank you for telling your mom about Cody before we got here today."

His green eyes studied her with a curious intensity. "Of course Sierra. I wanted to do what I could to make today one of those really good memories for you and for Cody."

She felt a warm glow flow through her at his words,

grateful that he was concerned for both of them. "Thank you."

Denver opened his mouth to say something, but suddenly he was hit in the shoulder by a snowball.

"Excuse me while I go pummel my brother." Denver grinned at her before quickly picking up a wad of snow and aiming it at his brother Wyatt.

"Looks like the two of them are going to be getting each other cold and wet by the time the day's over." Abby walked up to Sierra with a big grin on her face.

"Yeah. I guess that's what brothers do." Sierra turned to her good friend Abby.

"Well, I thought it would be good for the two of us to stick together, since we're surrounded by all these rowdy Callahan brothers." They both looked toward the base of the large hill just in time to see all seven brothers throwing snowballs at each other.

"Yeah, I'm glad you came today. It's really good to see you again." Sierra realized it had been months since she'd last seen her friend.

"Well, I have stuck closer to home but this time it's for a good reason." Abby's green eyes twinkled mysteriously.

Sierra's eyes grew big with a new awareness. "You're pregnant aren't you?"

"I am."

Sierra hugged her friend gently. "Oh, this is exciting. When do you expect the baby will be born?"

"Near as I can figure, early next summer." Abby chuckled. "But, Wyatt has forbidden me to do any horse riding or snow sledding. I know he's trying to protect the baby, but it sure limits my fun."

Sierra grinned at the grimace on her friend's face. "It's only until the baby's born, then you get back to doing all your favorite things."

"Yeah, I guess you're right. But, enough about me. I see Denver brought you here today with your son. I never knew who Cody's father was. But now seeing your son standing beside Denver today, it's so easy to tell they are father and son."

Guilt pricked at Sierra. "I'm sorry I never told you who Cody's dad was all the years we've been friends. I was so scared of somehow doing something wrong to make things worse for Cody, Grams, Granddad or Eban. So, I just kept silent."

"You don't have to explain, Sierra. I really do understand. But it amazes me how you were able to keep Cody under wraps without most folks in our small town knowing about him."

"Well I went to my Aunt Serena's home town, far away from where we live to give birth to Cody. And I went before my pregnancy was too far along. When I came back to Refuge Mountain, Cody was a couple weeks old and we just settled in quietly to life on the farm. I started working at the coffee shop again when Cody was nine months old. Grams or Eban have helped to take care of my son whenever I've needed to work."

"You amaze me. Single mom, hard worker and determined to protect your family. No wonder I adore you." Abby hugged her for a moment.

Sierra sighed happily. Abby had always been an understanding friend. They had helped each other through a lot of difficult moments throughout the years.

"I am very thankful for a wonderful friend like you, Abby." She felt a peace and contentment fill her.

Abby's eyes filled with questions. "Do you mind if I ask what happened to your relationship with Stuart?"

Sierra sighed heavily. "I'm sure you've already heard from someone in town that I broke up with Stuart."

Abby explained. "Well, Mellie who works as a secretary for Mr. Bitticombe in Stuart's office was at *A Goode Yarn* yesterday for our weekly crochet and knitting circle. She said Stuart was in a terrible mood for the last few days, ever since you broke up with him."

"You know how Mellie loves to chatter on and on about the latest news in town." Abby sighed. "But, I'd rather hear about what happened from you."

"Well, I went to his office a few days ago to surprise him. I was actually going to apologize for being so difficult and went there to surprise him." Sierra shivered as raw emotions swept over her.

"I opened the door to his office, and found Stuart holding another woman in his arms, kissing her. So, I gave him back the engagement ring and told him it was over between us."

Sierra shuddered as vivid memories returned at the shock of seeing Stuart kissing another woman.

"Well, all I can say is he doesn't deserve you if he's going to treat you like that." Abby squeezed her shoulder and smiled gently.

Sierra quickly wiped away a tear that created a new trail down one cheek. "Thanks. That's funny you should say that because that's the same thing Denver told me the other day."

"Oh? Do tell."

At Abby's teasing look, heat stained her neck and cheeks. "It's not at all what you're suggesting."

An expression of satisfaction shone in Abby's eyes and her smile was one of smug delight. "What was it that Shakespeare said? 'Methinks the lady doth protest too much.' I think Denver Callahan is as crazy about you as he ever was. And I think he's doing everything he can think of to try to win your heart."

For a moment she felt a sense of joy, until she remembered how he'd abandoned her. "Don't say that."

"Why not?" Abby leaned closer, looking her in the eyes. "Sierra, tell me what's wrong?"

To Sierra's dismay, moisture filled her eyes. Her words sounded hoarse and raw as they erupted from her lips. "It's just… it's just that I'm scared. I'm scared of my own attraction to Denver, but more than that I'm scared of starting a relationship with him again."

She expelled a long, slow breath. "He couldn't commit to marrying me years ago, so why should I believe that anything's changed. Why should I believe that he's changed?"

Abby nodded with eyes full of understanding. "That's a fair question, truly. And I understand that you're scared because of how hurt you were when he left town years ago without marrying you."

Sierra swallowed and nodded. "But?"

Abby offered a small smile. "But, how would you feel years from now if you didn't give Denver a chance? What if he truly has changed? What if he loves you and is willing to make that commitment to you and Cody?"

Her friend paused for a moment. "I think you owe it to yourself to find out. Instead of running away from him, give him a chance to prove himself to you."

Sierra swallowed and thought of how Denver seemed to be trying in the past week.

What if she did give Denver a chance? In many ways, that thought alternately thrilled and frightened her at the same time.

Sierra expelled a slow breath. "It's annoying how well you know me, you know that?" Abby only smiled as she waited. "All right I will give him a chance, so I won't regret it later on. But I don't think I'll be able to handle it, if he leaves me again."

"I don't believe you'll have reason to regret it." Abby glanced sideways before turning back to her. "And from the way he's staring at you right now, I'd say now is as good a time as any to give him a chance to prove it."

Sierra turned to see Denver standing not too far away, at the base of the mountain, with one arm resting on an upside down sled.

His head was cocked to one side and he had that devastating country star smile on his face. "Ready to join me?"

She tried to throttle the dizzying current racing through her. But heaven help her, every time she looked at him, the magnetic pull toward him was stronger.

"Coming." She called to Denver before she looked at Abby with a grimace. She heard the sound of Abby's laughter behind her as she walked toward Denver.

As she arrived at his side, he took her hand and they walked together up the mountain.

Denver placed the sled on the snow at the top of the mountain and climbed in so he was seated at the back. His long legs were stretched out in front of him, reaching to the front of the sled.

"I don't think there's room for me." Sierra whispered slowly.

Denver grabbed her hand and tugged her downwards. "Of course there is. You can sit down in front of me."

Hesitantly, she stepped onto the sled and seated herself in front of him carefully, so she wasn't leaning against him.

Denver didn't seem to think that was a good idea, because suddenly his arms surrounded her and he pulled her backwards so her back leaned up against his chest.

The warmth of his arms embraced her. Instead of fighting it, she took Abby's advice and settled back against him.

He whispered, his breath warm against her ear. "I've been waiting to go sledding with you. I remember how much fun we used to have years ago over by Potter's hill. I loved holding you in my arms back then and I still do today."

His words sent waves of excitement within her, but she pushed it down.

Instead she focused on how she was going to hang on. "What do I grab onto so I don't fall off?"

"Me, honey. You grab onto me and I'll hold onto you. I'll keep you safe."

Sierra felt like a breathless girl of eighteen again at his words. She cleared her throat pretending not to be affected. Placing her hands on his legs, she looked ahead and straight down the hill.

"Well then, I guess I'm as ready as I'll ever be."

"Good. Here goes." With his hands he pushed the sled forward until they started teetering over the edge of the large hill. Finally, the sled went over the edge and all of a sudden they were flying down the hill.

Denver's arms reached around her holding her close and she could feel his cheek against her hair.

Sierra screamed as they hit bumps along the way and flew even faster toward the bottom.

"It's okay. We're almost there. I've got you." Denver held her close until finally the sled came to a stop.

Sierra quickly wiped snow from her face, so she could see again. She turned to look behind her at Denver, and his large hand took her face and held it gently.

"I want to kiss you so badly, but I think we have a crowd of onlookers. I promise to come back to this moment later today." Denver whispered.

Sierra heard Cody run up to them calling her name.

"Mom, you went down the hill. I did too. I went sledding with Grandma, Uncle Dakota, Uncle Wyatt and with Uncle Hunter. It was so much fun going fast."

"I'm glad you've had fun." Sierra scurried out of the sled and hugged her son. Looking around she saw the rest of the Callahan family each going up and down the snow covered hill.

Cody's gaze switched between her and Denver. "Can I go on the sled with you and Denver, Mom?"

Sierra looked at Denver.

"Of course. Let's go." Denver chuckled and grabbed

Cody's hand. Sierra's heart lurched with a desperate longing. She hadn't dared to speak it out loud. But, the picture she saw with the three of them now, is what she wanted.

She wanted them to be a family. But she didn't know if it would be possible.

Even as old fears and insecurities rose up inside her, she remembered Abby's words.

What if he loves you and is willing to make that commitment to you and Cody? I think you owe it to yourself to find out. Instead of running away from him, give him a chance to prove himself and show that he loves you.

She could do this.

Hopefully, she wouldn't get her heart broken again in the process.

<h1 style="text-align:center">CHAPTER NINE</h1>

"IF HUNTER WOULD HAVE STOPPED TRYING to run me over every time we raced our sleds down the hill, I would have flown past him and beat him by a mile." Cole blurted out.

Hunter laughed loudly. "In your dreams."

Cole grinned and sipped his coffee, his eyes hooded while a half smile crept onto his face.

"You better watch it Hunter. I know that look on our youngest brother's face. He's plotting some sort of counter attack." Denver chuckled and turned to Sierra and winked.

She grinned, loving this large family and natural fun they had together.

They had all just finished eating the soup and sandwiches that the family's cook, Mrs. Garrett, had prepared and were drinking coffee.

Sierra turned to her son. The cup in his small hand slipped a little as he drank his apple juice. She took it out of his hand so it wouldn't spill, realizing that he was simply tired from the day's activities.

Her son had already been introduced to the puppies by his dad. He had played with the cute puppies for a long time before lunch. No wonder he was tired.

"Cody, did you have fun sledding today?" Denver's mom looked at her new grandson from her place at the head of the table.

Her son nodded, a tired smile on his face. "I did. Could we go sledding again sometime Grandma?"

Annie Callahan put her hand on her heart. "Oh Cody, I would absolutely love that. You are family and are welcome to come to the ranch whenever you want. We can go sledding, ride horses and many other things."

"But, right now you look a little tired out. If you want, you could go sit with the dogs in the family room. Most likely, Jack and Jill are lying down in their favorite spot by the fireplace."

"Oh goody. May I be excused Mom?"

"Sure you can, little bean. But first, you should let your Grandma know you are thankful for the food and then go wash your face and hands, okay?" Sierra used the napkin to wipe any crumbs from his mouth and hands.

"Okay." Cody ran to where his grandmother was seated and threw his arms around her. "Thank you for the food Grandma. I had fun with you today."

A tear rolled down Annie Callahan's cheek as she held

her new grandson in her arms. "I'm so happy you came today, Cody. I look forward to a great many new adventures with you."

Cody kissed his grandmother's cheek and then hurried off down the hallway to wash his hands.

Emotion flooded Sierra at the sight of Denver's mom's tears. She swallowed hard, trying to get control over her emotions.

She was grateful that Mrs. Callahan had accepted her new grandson so quickly.

Denver turned to her, a slow secret smile on his lips, letting her know he understood. He reached under the table and gently squeezed her hand. She offered a tentative smile in return, still feeling like the heady joy of the day was too good to be true.

"I should check on Cody. It's much too quiet in the other room." Sierra looked over at Denver's mom. "Thank you for lunch, Mrs. Callahan. If you'll excuse me, I think I should check on my son."

"You're welcome, Sierra. And it does sound quiet. He's probably with the dogs. Why don't we all go to the family room? It's more comfortable there." Annie Callahan stood to her feet and the family followed.

Sierra walked into the family room and looked in the direction of the large fireplace.

Her hand flew to her mouth in surprise when she saw Cody fast asleep in front of the fireplace. The two dogs were also sleeping one on either side of her son, like protective guardians.

Denver grinned and turned toward her, whispering. "Looks like our son has made some new furry friends."

"Yeah. I'm sure he's quite happy about it. Is it alright if he sleeps there for a little while?"

"Well, I was hoping he'd sleep for at least an hour." At her questioning look, he explained. "I would like to show you a new project I'm working on, if you don't mind riding horses to get there?"

"I don't mind." Sierra looked over at her son. "Should we take Cody with us?"

"No. He'll be fine here with my Mom. I'll talk to her." Denver walked over to his mom and Sierra followed.

"Mom, we were thinking of going riding for a little while. Would you mind keeping an eye on Cody?"

"Mind? I would love to watch over my grandson. Go. Have fun. We'll be fine here." Denver's mom reached over and squeezed Sierra's hand, her soft smile bringing with it a feeling of comfort and confidence that her son would be fine.

"Thank you." Sierra barely got the words out before Denver grabbed her hand and led her to the front door.

Hurriedly they put on their winter jackets and boots and headed out the door.

Denver grabbed her hand and led her to the large horse barn. "We'll take the two quarter horses that are mine."

Before long, Denver had saddled both quarter horses. One was a black sleek looking gelding and the other a bay mare with beautiful coloring.

He handed the reins of the bay mare to Sierra.

"What's her name?"

"Dancer. She's got a way of walking or trotting that is

very smooth. The name seemed appropriate." Denver grinned.

"I love the name Dancer." Sierra patted her mare's neck before she grabbed the horn and placed one foot in the stirrup of the saddle.

Suddenly Denver was behind her, whispering in her ear. "Let me help you up." His large hands encircled her waist. Her legs trembled at his touch and a tingling warmth flooded her body.

His grip tightened as he pushed her gently onto Dancer's broad back.

Sierra gripped the reigns with one hand and with the other held onto the saddle's horn.

It had been a long time since she'd ridden a horse, so she was a little uneasy in the saddle.

Denver got onto the black gelding with no problem and turned its head toward the large open sliding barn door. Sierra followed with her mare and soon they were walking the horses on a snow covered trail that led them to the river that was on Callahan ranch land.

It was a beautiful sunny day and the air was brisk and cool from the recent snow.

"So where are we headed, or is that a secret?" Sierra questioned, admiring the picture Denver made with his black cowboy hat, wide shoulders and lean muscled legs as he sat comfortably on his black gelding.

He turned to look at her and their eyes locked. A delightful shiver ran through her as he gave her a smile that sent her pulse racing.

"You'll recognize the place when we get there."

Sierra nodded, and couldn't help but feel a curious excitement building inside her.

What did he mean she would recognize the place? Her mind drifted back to seven years ago, during their dating years. They had come to the Callahan ranch a few times, but it had only been to see his parents or to go riding.

After a while, they reached the river and led the horses along the bank of the river.

Seeing the bridge up ahead, she immediately recognized the road.

"I'm sorry Sierra. We need to cross the bridge to get to the place I'm taking you." Denver slowed his horse, so he was riding next to her.

Sierra swallowed back emotion as she recognized the road. Riverview road was the same road where her parents had died in that car accident years ago.

With a trembling voice she said. "It's okay. We're only going over the bridge and you're with me, so everything will be okay." Sierra spoke more to convince herself than for any other reason.

"Are you truly okay?" Denver whispered and reached over to hold her hand. The compassion in his green eyes was her undoing.

"It's still difficult thinking about the death of my parents. I know, I should be over it by now, it's been years." Hurriedly she swiped away a stray tear, angry that she still cried about her loss.

"I don't think you ever truly get over losing a loved one. I think a person begins to heal, but there will always be this missing hole in your heart I think."

She nodded and swallowed convulsively. "You're wise

Denver. I think that's true about the missing hole. I still miss my mom and dad. But the good memories are what I hold onto. For instance, I remember my mom taking me horseback riding when we would visit my grandparent's farm. She loved animals like I did and it became our special time together."

"That's a great memory to have of your mom." There was a gentle softness in his voice.

She turned to him and spoke in a broken whisper. "Thanks for understanding Denver."

He simply squeezed her hand again. They walked the horses up the embankment to the top, where the road met the bridge.

Sierra couldn't help but stare back a mile, to the spot where Riverview road had a sharp bend.

She pointed a finger to the place. "See that sharp corner about a mile back?"

He nodded.

"The policeman who investigated the accident said the speed of the vehicle and the sharp curve combined with the fact that the car was an antique is what caused my parents' accident." Sierra sighed heavily as she remembered Grams talking to the blue uniformed man the day he had arrived at their door.

"What? Sounds like perhaps the police were tired of investigating and so they figured out a simple explanation for what happened." There was an edge to Denver's voice as he spoke.

"What do you mean?" Sierra questioned, a crease forming between her brows.

"Well, other people drive their cars on this road all the

time. So how have they managed to drive around that sharp curve without their vehicles sliding over the edge of the steep cliff?"

Sierra nodded. "I don't really understand it either. I remember at the time of the accident, Granddad said he thought it was strange that the police didn't seem to do a lot of investigation into the accident. He talked to them about it, but they were convinced the accident was an open and shut case. The case was closed within a month."

Denver shook his head, sighing with exasperation.

"We did keep the car though. It's still on Granddad and Gram's farm. It was the same car Granddad used when he began courting Grams way back in the day. When my dad finished high school, Granddad gave the car to my dad. So when the car accident happened, Granddad brought the car back to the farm."

"Interesting. You still have the car from the accident?"

Sierra nodded. "Yes. It hasn't been touched since the accident. But I don't like to look at it, so years ago Granddad covered the car with a tarp."

A shadow of annoyance hovered in his eyes and he clenched his mouth tighter. "It doesn't seem right. I'm going to do some asking around."

Sierra sighed. "Denver, they closed the case years ago. I understand your frustration, but most likely you won't find anything new even if you dig around."

"I understand how you feel, Sierra. Call it a gut feeling." Denver smiled at her before guiding his horse in the direction of the bridge. She wondered what he was thinking or planning.

But at the moment, it seemed he was done talking about that.

"All right." She sighed. Her natural inquiring mind wondered what he was up to. But, truth be told, she didn't want to continue dwelling on her parent's accident. It hurt too much to go through round after round of painful memories.

Sighing, she nudged her horse forward until she was beside him. They walked the horses for another stretch of road before Denver guided the horse onto a dirt road. The path took them towards a hill that overlooked the large river below.

"How much farther until we reach our destination?"

Denver finally stopped his horse at the base of the hill, with tall poplar trees behind them and in front of them, far below, was the river.

"We've arrived. So tell me, does this place look familiar to you?" An easy smile rested on his mouth and a new contentment shone on his face.

Sierra looked around, noticing the hill behind them and the rushing river below. For a moment she was convinced she did not recognize the place until suddenly she spotted the old trappers log cabin hidden in the trees.

She turned to him, her voice breathless. "This is your land that you inherited from your dad."

"Yeah." Denver expelled a breath. His sigh of contentment said it all.

They looked at each other and smiled in earnest.

"It's beautiful here, Denver." Sierra breathed in the fresh mountain air. "I remembered this place when I saw that old trapper's cabin. You rescued me from the river years ago and carried me up that steep embankment, soaking wet and half drowned, into that old cabin. I could never forget what you did for me. You saved my life that day."

His mouth curved with tenderness. "It's enough for me to have you by my side again, with that smile on your beautiful face."

At his heartfelt words, she felt wrapped in an invisible warmth.

She watched as Denver climbed off his horse and tethered him. Sierra began to get off her mare, when she felt Denver's hands on her waist. He slowly slid her down to the ground, his arms wrapped around her waist.

Her heart hammered in her ribs at being held so closely in his arms.

"Thanks." She looked up into his green eyes and her heart melted. His gaze was soft as a caress and traveled over her face, searching her eyes.

Slowly, he leaned down and touched his lips to her forehead.

It was a gentle kiss that left her wanting more.

Sierra was oddly disappointed when he pulled away from her so quickly. It didn't make sense, but her feelings for him were intensifying. Her feelings didn't have anything to do with reason.

Sierra found herself studying his profile as he pulled away.

If she didn't know better, she could have convinced herself that this confident man — this well known country singer — was a little nervous.

But, that couldn't be right. She was sure she was imagining things. Ever since she'd known Denver, he'd been so confident, so sure of himself.

His voice was unsteady and he swallowed quickly. Holding his hand out, she placed her small one in his.

"Come with me. There's something I want to show you."

He quickly tethered her mare alongside his gelding and they walked farther up the hill. Trees surrounded them until they arrived at the top of the hill where there were acres of flat ground.

Her hand felt safe and secure in his much larger one. It was incredible to her that the mere touch of his hand sent a warming shiver through her.

Sierra tried to change her focus and looked around the acres of flat ground and the view of the valley below.

As her gaze scanned the area, she caught sight of a large building being constructed.

"What are you building?" Without thinking, she walked toward the construction site so she could get a better view.

His boots crunched the snow behind her. "It's a house I had designed together with an architect friend I know. I finally got the general contractor to begin the project last week."

She walked closer, noticing the massive construction frame. "This will be a very large house."

"Yeah. I love the idea of having a lot of space for a family and for guests who come to visit." Denver stepped onto the wood flooring. "Let's walk around and I'll show you the design of the house." Reaching one hand down, he pulled her up so she stood on the newly constructed floorboards.

"So this large area is to be the kitchen and it leads into a large dining room. Off to the corner is a smaller break-fast nook which will have a large window to look at the valley below." Denver took her on a tour to show her how the house would be designed.

"There will be ten bedrooms upstairs and downstairs with a private bathroom in each room. There will also be two large offices, a workout gym, a library, a smaller family room and of course a large great room." He pointed to the places each of the rooms would be located.

Sierra walked beside him until they stood where the great room would be located.

"This will be an incredible view right here of the miles and miles of land stretching across the valley below this hill." Sierra stood motionless picturing the large windows where a person could see for miles.

"What do you think of the overall house design?" Denver stood so close to her that his thigh brushed against her own. He gently placed one hand lightly on her shoulder as they both looked at the view below.

Her wildly beating heart was the only sound audible.

She turned slightly to answer his question. "I love it. It's the perfect combination of open concept, but still keeping enough space for privacy. And with all the bedrooms you have included, you will have lots of room to entertain. This will be a great house for you. I hope I'll be invited to the housewarming party."

Denver turned and gently his arms encircled her. "Oh,

you definitely will be. Without you there, the party wouldn't be worth having."

His whispered words brought a rush of pink to her cheeks. She didn't know exactly what he meant, but he made it sound like she was important.

A warmth flooded her senses at his words of appreciation.

Her skin tingled as his hands explored the hollows of her back. Even through her jacket, she could feel his gentle strength.

Denver's green eyes searched hers and then he looked downward to focus on her lips.

A thrill of anticipation and fear touched her at the same time. She placed her hands on his chest intending to push him away, when all of a sudden Abby's words rang in her ears. Instead of running away from him, give him a chance to prove himself to you.

So, rather than pushing him away, Sierra relaxed, sinking into his cushioning embrace.

His lips came coaxingly down on hers and she drank in the sweetness of his kiss.

Slowly, she slipped her arms around his neck and kissed him back. Encouraged, he pulled her closer. There was a dreamy intimacy to his kiss now. She felt her knees weaken as his mouth caressed hers.

All too soon, Denver pulled his lips away from hers. "I could kiss you forever. But that will have to wait."

He stopped and took a deep, unsteady breath and took a step back. Straightening his black cowboy hat on his head again, he touched one finger to the tip of his hat. It was an old fashioned gesture that she adored.

"Thank you for coming with me today."

At his intense gaze and whispered words her heart swelled with a feeling she had thought long since dead.

Softly she replied. "Thanks for inviting me. I really enjoyed coming here with you and spending the day together."

Denver grinned and reached out, catching her hand in his. "Well, we should be getting back. Our son might be awake and wondering where we are."

She nodded back at him without speaking, but her emotions felt deeply when he said the words, *our son*. She really hoped he meant to be committed to loving Cody and spending time with him.

Sierra hurried after him as he walked to the makeshift entrance of the construction site. He jumped to the ground first. Then his strong hands circled her waist and lifted her down, swirling her around in a circle.

Sierra giggled at his spur-of-the-moment fun.

Her hat flew off her head and Denver set her gently on the ground.

Picking up her hat, he placed it on her head and kissed her cheek.

Grabbing her hand, they walked together to the horses.

As they rode home, Sierra mentally rehearsed all the special moments of their day together.

She had surprised herself and loved spending the day with Denver. Old feelings for him, which she'd been convinced were long dead, were beginning to revive again.

A crease formed between her brows as she remembered Aunt Serena's words.

Yesterday, Sierra had a quick coffee with her Aunt and had agreed to her offer to be a silent partner in buying the coffee shop. When her Aunt asked what she was doing for the weekend, she told her about spending the day with Denver Callahan.

When Sierra had commented that she hoped the day went well, Aunt Serena had responded with a touch of cynicism. *I don't know why you would want to spend time with him. I never did like him much, especially after you came to live with me pregnant and alone. I really don't think you should let him back into your life Sierra. He's already proven to you once that he's a love 'em and leave 'em kind of guy. I'd be very careful to guard my heart around him if I were you.*

Looking over at Denver riding beside her with that tender smile on his face, made her believe Aunt Serena had been wrong about him.

Maybe they had both been wrong about him.

Maybe, he was transforming into the man she had longed for him to be all those years ago.

Maybe this time things would be different between them.

The nagging in the back of her mind refused to be stilled, but she pushed it back.

Maybe this time there would be a second chance at love for both of them.

enver

DRIVING ONTO HIS LAND, Denver was once again so grateful to his Dad for giving him this little piece of heaven on earth as his inheritance.

This was the first time he'd been back to the construction site since he'd been here a week ago.

He parked his truck for a moment, amazed at how much work had been accomplished since then. The walls were up and it looked like they were adding the roof today.

Denver had asked Henry, his General Contractor, to hire as many workers as necessary so that the house would be built as soon as possible.

The guest house that was located a few hundred yards away from the main house was further along. Today, a wood craftsman was already building the kitchen shelves and handmade shelving in the bathroom and family room.

Henry assured him that the guest house would be finished just before Christmas.

A smile formed on his lips as he remembered Sierra's reaction to the new house. He thought of how her eyes lit up when he gave her a quick tour of where everything was going to be in the house. She had really loved the view from the planned location of the great room.

His confidence spiralled upward.

It took all his willpower to hold back from telling Sierra that this house design was basically the same idea she'd had when they were dating.

Denver had written her ideas in his journal years ago. Just a few months ago when he'd met with his architect, the blueprint for the house had come to life.

But, he hadn't said anything. He sensed it wasn't the right time yet to ask her to marry him. Right now, Sierra was like a wounded filly who had been abused by her handler one too many times.

She was still hesitant and unsure of him.

He needed to prove himself to her that this time he meant to stay with her and their son.

Regret washed over him again at the way he'd suddenly left her years ago. He'd promised to marry her, but in the end he'd chosen to run away instead. Deacon words came back to him. You can't play heartfelt songs like you just did about love, and then run away from it yourself.

It was true. He had written all sorts of country songs

about love and committed love, but had run away from making a commitment to the one woman he loved.

Well, that was about to change.

But, first he needed to show Sierra he'd become a changed man.

As he drove the road that led to their small town, he was reminded that his time co-hosting the Christmas Fair with Sierra was almost over.

He wanted to ask Sierra to go with him on a very special date before their time at the studio everyday was done.

An idea popped into his mind just as he arrived at the television studio.

It would be the perfect date.

The loud ringing of his smartphone interrupted his thoughts.

"Denver here."

"It's Jake Davis from Davis Investigative Services. Just wanted to give you a quick update."

"Jake, good to hear from you." Denver remembered it was early last week that he'd asked Jake to search for more information on the accident that caused John and Amelia Baxter's car accident. He wanted to do what he could to make things right for Sierra and her grandparents. "Did you find any new information?"

"Yes, as it turns out. But, it might not be anything important."

"Let's hear it."

"One of Baxter's old neighbors, who has since moved away, remembered that day because it was Thanksgiving Day. She recalled seeing a boy who looked to be about thirteen years old. He was walking behind the fence line on Baxter's farm and went straight into the garage. It was daylight, so she assumed the Baxter's knew him and so she didn't say anything."

"Did you find out his name?"

"No. I'll need to do some more digging. Sorry, we didn't find anything useful. We'll keep digging into this story and see what we discover. I'll keep you informed of any new developments."

"Thanks Jake. I just want to finally uncover the real cause of Sierra's parents' car accident all those years ago, so Sierra and her family can put it behind them once and for all."

"I understand Denver. I'm on it. Talk to you soon."

Denver hung up the phone, his thoughts swirling after hearing the new information.

Who was this boy and why had he been at Baxter's farm years ago?

Maybe it was just a fluke that he was there at all on that fateful day years ago. Right now, they didn't have any answers.

However, Denver was glad that Jake Davis was investigating matters so they would finally uncover the truth.

SIERRA LEFT THE COFFEE SHOP, hurrying down the street towards the television studio.

Checking her wristwatch she figured she would make it just in time. She walked faster.

Her thoughts were filled with so many new and exciting things that were happening in her life lately.

Earlier this week they had signed papers at Aunt Serena's lawyer's office to buy *The Little Bean Cafe.*

Her dream of owning the coffee shop had come true. Mrs. Jenkins, her old boss, had been quite happy to sell the coffee shop.

However, she had whispered to Sierra. *Remember you can come to me with any questions or concerns. We're friends and I'll do what I can to help you in whatever way I can.*

Tears pricked at the back of Sierra's eyes at the memory. Her old boss had always been so kind and generous to her. She would remember Mrs. Jenkin's kind words.

Aunt Serena had told her she would organize all the paperwork for their business with her accountant so that everything would run like clockwork.

She appreciated her aunt taking care of little details like that, because it gave her more time to take care of ordering the products they needed and taking care of their workers.

Sierra hurried into the Studio and their makeup artist worked quickly to get her ready to be on camera.

As soon as she sat next to Denver on set, he whispered. "You look beautiful as usual."

Heat stained her neck and cheeks at his compliment. Ever since they had spent the day together a week ago, Denver seemed to find some way to say something nice, or to help her in some way.

"Thank you Denver." She whispered and looked back at her notes feeling his eyes on her.

Much like it had been last weekend.

Being with Denver at the Callahan ranch had been so much fun. Being by his side to see his building project had given her a new perspective of Denver.

In her mind, she'd pictured him as the careless country music star, instead she'd seen a thoughtful, considerate and gentle cowboy whose first concern had been for her.

This was the kind of man she'd dreamed of marrying years ago.

But that man had left her. This new man had returned, but she still didn't know if the change was real.

But, Sierra had promised her friend Abby that she would give him a chance.

And so she would. But she could admit that there was a part of her heart she held back.

Maybe, in time that would change.

Memories returned of walking through the beautiful layout that Denver had for his house. For some reason it captivated her. In fact, it was a house design she would have liked for herself. She could imagine having a beautiful view of the valley every morning.

But she didn't have the money for that kind of dream.

So, for the time being, she would have to use her imagination to take her to the places she couldn't see in real life.

"I want to ask you something after the show today, okay?" Denver whispered.

Anxiety knotted inside her, but she nodded quickly. "Sure."

For the next hour they co-hosted the tenth day of the Christmas Fair, which included ten young school age boys from their town dancing their own version of *Ten Lords A Leaping.*

Sierra couldn't stop smiling after the show was finished.

Those boys were so cute in their regency style costumes with the black tall hats. She was so impressed by the creativity that came out of different dance clubs, schools and from other folks around their small town.

Folding up her papers, suddenly she felt herself being turned slowly in her swivel chair until she met Denver's intense green eyes.

Before his appealing smile, her defenses melted away.

"Would you be interested in going to supper with me? It's a place that holds some of the best memories for me and I'd like to share it with you." His mouth curved with tenderness and unconsciously she smiled easily in return.

He rested his hand on hers. The mere touch of his hand sent a warming shiver through her.

"Sure. I'd like that." Sierra whispered in return. "I won't be home until late this afternoon, as I have an appointment with my mother's lawyer."

One eyebrow was raised in question. "Oh? That sounds intriguing."

"Yeah. I'll explain more later. But right now, I should probably go so I'm not late." Sierra stood to her feet. His nearness sent her pulses spinning. She was so tempted to step into his arms, that she quickly took a step back.

"I'll pick you up at six?"

"Yes. I look forward to it." Sierra smiled and turned, hurrying out of the television studio.

The appointment with her mother's lawyer took a few

hours, but she still had time to check in at the coffee shop before she picked up Cody and drove back home.

She was just putting the finishing touches on her makeup when Denver arrived at the door.

Eban gave her one of those looks that said I hope you know what you're doing as she answered the door. Her brother had always been protective of her, ever since their parents' accident.

Sierra smiled confidently at Eban, hoping to reassure him that she would be alright.

She gave Cody a quick kiss. "Be good for Grams."

"I will Mom. Will I see Denver when he brings you back home?"

"I think you'll be asleep by then, little bean."

"Then I will give him a hug now." Cody ran to his dad and threw his arms around his waist.

Denver put his arms gently around his son. He looked over at Sierra, and her heart turned over at the moisture she saw in Denver's eyes. He kissed the top of his son's head. "Thank you, Cody."

"Mom says I give the best hugs, so I wanted to give you one too." Cody stepped away and ran back to Grams.

They said goodbye to everyone and as Denver helped her into the truck, he said. "That little guy is pretty amazing.

She felt a warm glow pass throughout her body at his words. She knew their son was amazing, but it felt so good to hear him say it.

"I think so too."

She smiled happily as Denver drove down the highway.

It was only thirty minutes later, when he surprised her by turning into the cafe where she worked as a teenager, Rusty's Café and Bar.

Sierra's eyes widened and Denver grinned as he opened the truck door on her side and helped her out.

Sierra wore a long flowing navy skirt, a pink blouse with her long strawberry blond hair flowing loose in thick waves down to her waist.

He felt incredibly lucky that this beautiful woman was by his side tonight.

Turning to her, he noticed her wide eyes. "Are you surprised?"

"I am. But it will be good to see Rusty again. It's been a long time since I last saw him."

Denver placed his hand on the small of her back as they walked inside the double doors of the Cafe.

"Looks like they have a local country band singing tonight." The music played softly in the background as they made their way to a table for two in the far corner.

They had only sat down for a minute, when Rusty himself walked over to their table.

"Well I'll be. If it isn't Denver Callahan and Sierra Baxter." Rusty's voice was chuckling and hearty just as she remembered. He clapped Denver on the shoulder.

"We wanted to see if the cafe was still running, Rusty." Denver grinned.

"We're still going strong, Denver. But there's not so many who did as well as you did."

"I'm glad to be back, Rusty. I'll never forget how you helped me get my start."

"Ah, Denver, you know you've always been like a son

to me. I still remember how you would tag along with your mother when she worked for me all those years ago." He looked at Sierra.

"Back then the rules were a little more relaxed." Rusty winked at her before turning back to speak to Denver. "Some evenings, when there was a band that didn't show up, your mother would play guitar and sing."

Rusty sighed. "I'll always remember seeing that happy glow on your face when you would hear her sing. Your mother knew it too, which is why when she was sick, she made me promise to do what I could to help you."

"You were a godsend to both mama and myself." Denver squeezed the older man's shoulder.

"Well, I don't know. The two of you helped me just as much as I helped you." Rusty reached for a hanky in his pocket and wiped his nose. "But enough of me, blabbing on and on. What can I get to drink for the two of you?"

"We'll start with two iced teas, Rusty. I'm driving you know, so I can't get too carried away." Denver grinned.

"Coming right up." Rusty hurried away behind the counter at the bar. Denver turned to look at her.

Sierra couldn't help but mist up a little at the story Rusty shared. "I didn't realize Rusty was such an important part of your life when you were little."

"Yeah, mama worked for him, but he really did treat me like a son. I really do owe him for all the help he gave me as I started playing and singing my songs back then." Denver sighed.

"Maybe you should sing a little tonight, since you're here."

Denver shrugged. "Maybe. We'll see how the night goes."

The waitress arrived to take their order for food.

He leaned over and reached out his hand to hers. "Tell me first about your week or your day. I want to hear what is happening with you, Sierra."

The way his fingers played with hers, sent tingles shooting up and down her arm.

"Well, I've had an exciting week as I've just bought *The Little Bean Cafe* from Mrs. Jenkins."

"Good for you Sierra. You'll be a big success. That's a big investment."

Sierra nodded. "Well, to be fair I wasn't able to do it by myself. My mother's sister Aunt Serena, offered to be a silent partner. But we were approved for the business loan. It feels good to fulfill my dream of owning a coffee shop."

"I'm glad for you Sierra." Denver sipped his iced tea before asking. Just then the waitress set plates filled with their food order on the table.

"You say your mother's sister is a financial partner?"

Sierra nodded. "Yes. My aunt's name is Serena Jeffries."

A furrow formed between her brows.

Denver squeezed her hand. "Why the frown? What are you thinking?"

"I was just thinking that I met with my mother's lawyer, William Hamilton, today. He had sent a letter early this week asking me to meet him at his office."

"Did he want something in particular?"

"Yes. To my surprise, my mother had set up a trust fund for myself and my brother, Eban. We receive it when we turn twenty-five years old. He said it's a substantial amount of money."

"Since my twenty-fifth birthday is in five days, Mr. Hamilton wanted to meet with me a few days early to tell me about my inheritance. He also wanted to give me my mother's journals and said my mom had put them in his care for safekeeping all these years. Then he asked if I would meet back at his office on my birthday. So I agreed."

"That's good news, right?"

"Yes, it is good news. But, I wish I knew why my mother would ask her lawyer to keep her private journals. It all seems so strange."

Denver shook his head silently. "I don't understand that either, unless there were some people who your mother didn't trust?"

They continued eating in silence until they finished their plate of food.

Sierra couldn't stop thinking about her mom and the reasons she would give her journals to her lawyer.

"Maybe there was." A crease formed between her brows. "Well, hopefully more answers will show up as I read my mom's journals. It will be so wonderful to get to know who she really was ." Tears welled up in her eyes and she blinked them quickly away.

"Yes it will, Sierra. I know it was comforting to read my dad's letter the lawyer gave to me after he passed away. After reading my dad's words, I found I understood more about who he was and who I was."

"It was encouraging. I hope you discover something similar when you read your mother's journals." Denver's thumb caressed the smooth skin on the top of her hand. It was a comforting gesture and something she really needed.

"Thanks, Denver."

The band in the small Cafe stopped playing as Rusty stood up to the microphone.

"We have an unexpected visitor at Rusty's Cafe and Bar tonight. He's a man most of you will be familiar with. Maybe if we encourage him, he'll play some of those top ten country music hits for us tonight. Denver what do you say?"

Folks scattered throughout the cafe and bar clapped and called out Denver's name.

Sierra watched Denver's cheeks turn a ruddy red at the unexpected attention. She was surprised. She would have expected Denver to be used to the continual attention from fans, but perhaps he appreciated his privacy just as much as she did.

He nodded and sent them a smile. He turned to her and whispered. "I'll play a few songs and be right back, okay?" His eyes clung to hers, as if needing her support.

She nodded quickly, surprised. "I can't wait to hear you sing, Denver. I'll be here waiting."

He walked to the stage. The band leader handed Denver his own guitar to play.

With a nod of thanks to everyone in the place, he sat on the stool and began to play and sing some of the songs he'd written over the years.

The audience was held captive.

Some danced to his music, some people sang along and others like Sierra sat motionless, listening.

Sierra was especially captivated by the last song he sang. She remembered hearing this song as one of the first ones played on the radio station.

Denver gazed focused on her and it seemed like he poured his heart out as he sang. *So many wasted years and wasted nights. So many years lost between us.*

Denver's low voice slowly breathed out the last line of the song. *Now I only dream of you. I don't love nobody like you.*

As his voice faded away, his fans erupted into applause.

Denver said a whispered thanks into the microphone and gave the band leader his guitar back.

As Denver walked back to their table, slow country music crooned in the background.

Sierra hardly noticed, because she was so moved by Denver's last song and even more so by the bold intensity of his green eyes.

Reaching the table, he held out his hand silently asking her to dance.

Her hand shook a little as she placed her small hand in his large one. He walked with her to the dance floor, and placed both hands on her waist. She rested her hands on his shoulders and looked into his eyes.

The smoldering flame she saw in Denver's eyes startled her. A tingling began in the pit of her stomach and a familiar spark of excitement returned like it always did whenever she was close to Denver.

Her emotions melted as he stoked a gently growing fire inside her.

"I really loved the songs you sang, Denver. Especially that last one. The words brought tears to my eyes." The whispered words rushed out of her mouth before she had a chance to filter them.

Denver stepped closer and clasped her body tightly to his. She raised her arms, placing her hands lightly around his neck. They danced cheek to cheek in slow motion.

He kissed the side of her head.

Then he whispered, his breath warm against her ear. "I'm glad the song moved you sweetheart, because I wrote that song just for you."

A soft gasp escaped her.

The implication of what he was telling her hit her. The song he sang had been one of the first songs he'd ever written. It was a song of regret of the wasted years between him and the woman he loved and a simple declaration that there was nobody else that he loved but her.

Denver pulled back just enough so he could look into her eyes. Her eyes had widened and she stared wordlessly at him, her heart pounding.

The tenderness in his expression amazed her.

"It's true. You've always been my one and only." Despite his smile she sensed his vulnerability.

His words struck a vibrant chord in her, because she felt a similar longing deep inside.

Yet, something held her back from saying the three words she believed he wanted to hear.

Instead of speaking, she stood on tiptoe and kissed his lips softly. Then she turned her head, resting it against his chest.

His heartbeat throbbed in her ears.

He embraced her closely and she could hear his whispered words. "The game is not played fairly, Sierra."

She could feel the smile in his teasing words. "You'll have to wait until later so I can give you repayment in kind."

As his words hinted at kisses, her blood pounded in her brain, leapt from her heart and made her knees tremble.

She enjoyed being in his arms as Denver held her close for the next dance too. She drank in the comfort of his nearness, surprised by the intensity of her own longing for him.

Could there be a possibility for a second chance at love for them?

Her heart wanted to scream yes, but her logical mind held doubts that this new closeness between her and Denver would last.

CHAPTER ELEVEN

ierra

SHE HUMMED along to a love song on the radio as she drove to the coffee shop.

Memories of her evening two days ago with Denver Callahan returned and she exhaled a long sigh of contentment.

He'd made good on his promise to give her repayment in kind for the brief kiss she'd given him. His toe-curling kisses he'd given her later, still caused her to feel as if she were floating.

Her heart was still fluttering wildly in her breast as she parked her car and walked into *The Little Bean Cafe*.

Turning her mind toward the day's work, she spoke to the baristas and waitresses who worked the early morning shift.

"Just to let you all know we're expecting a shipment just before noon today, so if two of you would be available to help with that?"

After two workers volunteered, she continued telling everyone about a couple of small changes she was making. "So, that's it everyone. Thanks so much for your hard work." Sierra smiled and started working on the order for supplies she needed for the rest of the week.

In the middle of her tallying the numbers she needed, her smartphone buzzed with an incoming text.

"Hey, Sierra. How's your morning going at the coffee shop today?"

"Good. We're staying real busy which is just what we want. How are you doing Aunt Serena?" Sierra was surprised her aunt was texting her this early in the morning.

"I'm a little worried about our coffee shop to be honest."

Sierra's heart plummeted to her toes. "Why, what's wrong?"

"Simply put, we're not making enough profit. Have you been giving a bunch of discounts or doing something else differently in the past week?"

Sierra thought back to everything she'd done in the past week. "Nothing has changed. I can tell you I have been using the same method for pricing and discounts that I learned from my old boss, Mrs. Jenkins. And from what I've seen from this past week, the coffee shop has been just as busy as when Lottie owned it."

"Well then, something else must be wrong. My accountant tells me I need to see greater profit for this coffee shop, or this business is too risky. It's not about you, my dear, it's just good business sense. We'll talk again soon."

"Let me see if there are some changes I can make around here to increase our profit margins. Talk to you soon."

Sierra signed off, and ran a shaky hand through her hair. Next, she went through all their statements since they bought the coffee shop, looking at their revenues and expenses.

She spent the next two hours going over the books for the business.

When she tallied the total, it seemed like the profits they were making were in line with what Mrs. Jenkins said were normal.

She wondered what was wrong. Deciding she needed some advice, she dialled her old boss's phone number.

"Mrs. Jenkins? This is Sierra."

"Oh Sierra. How nice to hear from you. I'm sitting on my deck, enjoying my coffee this sunny morning. You should come over." Sierra smiled at the chuckle on the other end of the phone line.

"Well actually, I was going to ask if I could pop by and talk to you after lunch. There are some questions I have about the coffee shop, that I'm hoping you can help me out with."

"Of course, my dear. I'll be at home, whenever you get here."

"Thanks. I'll be there soon." Sierra hung up the phone and sighed heavily. What was wrong? Could she be failing as a new business owner already when she had just started?

Sierra finished the work she had to do that morning, and then drove over to Mrs. Jenkins' house.

Her home was located at the other end of the same street where Aunt Serena had leased a house.

Large oak and pine trees had grown between the beautiful Victorian homes that lined the street.

Sierra parked her car and walked up to Mrs. Jenkins' home. Before she could knock, her old boss opened the door.

"Come in, Sierra." Mrs. Jenkins led the way to the kitchen where she poured them each a glass of lemonade.

"Let's go sit on the deck so we can enjoy this fine day and have a nice chat at the same time." Lottie Jenkins opened the patio doors, where they settled into soft lounge chairs.

Sierra was amazed that from the deck they could see almost all of the neighboring homes, including Aunt Serena's house.

Sierra took a sip of the lemonade. "This is nice and cool for this warm day."

"It is isn't it?" Mrs. Jenkins set down her lemonade and turned toward her. "So, you said you had a question or a concern that you wanted help with."

"Yes, I do." Sierra explained about the text she got from her Aunt and her concerns that the coffee shop wasn't making hardly any profit. "So before I came here I went through the revenue and expenses ever since we bought the business from you. I'm not an accountant, but I wrote down the numbers."

Sierra took the paper out of her pocket and handed it over. Mrs. Jenkins read through the outgoing expenses and revenues for each day since her and Aunt Serena had bought the business from her.

"You know after looking at this, I can't see too many differences from what my profit margins were at the coffee shop every day. It looks to be very similar to my own experience."

Sierra sighed. "Then, I don't know how to find the problem. Do you have any thoughts on other places I should look to solve this problem, Mrs. Jenkins?"

"Well, my dear. I've come to realize that in business, the money either adds up or it doesn't. So if the problem isn't with incoming revenue or with the outgoing expenses, then the next place I'd go to find answers is with the person who handles your books."

"Aunt Serena says she takes my reports that I give her, to the accountant weekly." A crease formed between her brows as she realized she needed to get to the bottom of this. "I'll need to ask Aunt Serena who her accountant is so I can talk to him."

Mrs. Jenkins squeezed her hand lightly. "Let me tell you a little secret that will help you in business my dear. Always keep close tabs on which hand — no matter how many — handles your money."

"Whether it's the tax man, the accountant, a partner or a bank. It's important that you always keep a close watch on every single dime that goes through your business. That's how you will make a success of it and also be a good steward of the business the good Lord saw fit to give you."

Sierra thought on her words, and realized she really hadn't been keeping tabs on much of anything besides ordering supplies and talking to the workers.

"I haven't been doing a very good job of keeping track

of all aspects of this business. It all feels very new to me, but that's no excuse. Thanks for your advice. I will begin to keep track of everything that's going on. I really appreciate your good business sense."

"Of course my dear. I learned the hard way at the beginning, so if I can make things easier for you, then I'm happy to do so."

After they caught up on a few other details of each other's lives, Mrs. Jenkins walked Sierra out the door.

Sierra turned to walk to her car, when she saw Stuart's car drive up to Aunt Serena's home at the other end of the street.

Sierra inhaled quickly.

"What is it, Sierra?"

"I just saw Stuart's car park at Aunt Serena's home. He's talking with her now." She could feel the blood drain away from her face. "What is he up to? We are no longer engaged to be married, so why would he be visiting my aunt?"

"Well, Stuart is an accountant. Perhaps, your aunt hired him to handle her tax forms?" Mrs. Jenkins' suggestion seemed to ring true.

"Or maybe Stuart is the accountant that is responsible for writing down the details of the weekly revenue and expenses for the coffee shop. Maybe he's cooking the books, so to speak." She knew Stuart was mad at her for giving him back her ring.

"As a way to get back at you for ending your engagement?"

Sierra fought to control her swirling emotions. "I wouldn't put it past him."

Sadly, that was the truth. The more she had got to know Stuart, especially during their brief engagement, the more she realized how volatile and unpredictable his emotions really were. She could picture him finding great satisfaction in causing her business to fail and ruining her.

She tried to hide her inner misery from Mrs. Jenkins' probing stare.

"Maybe that's true." Her boss nodded. "But if I were you, I wouldn't confront him without having the facts. However, hiring someone who could search into the matter, would be a good idea."

"I believe I'll do that." Sierra moved restlessly as she tried to digest this new possibility. She quickly hugged the older lady before she turned to leave. "You've been a big help to me today. Thank you, Mrs. Jenkins."

"Anytime my dear. And do stop by again. I love having visitors."

"I will." Sierra waved to her old boss and drove away, her thoughts on what she'd learned this day.

Sierra decided to talk to Denver. It would be helpful to get his advice on how to handle this. He had shown that he had her best interests at heart.

His tender care of her changed something in her heart — something that she never thought possible: she was beginning to love and trust him again.

DENVER DROVE the dirt road that led to Baxter's farm.

He was excited to bring a surprise gift to his son. He only hoped Sierra wouldn't mind.

Parking his truck near the garage, he noticed that the sliding doors to the double bay garage were wide open.

Hearing tools thudding on the ground, he walked inside the garage. Eban was bent over looking inside the hood of his truck.

"I see you're hard at work." Denver walked casually toward Sierra's brother, hoping to have a conversation with him.

Glancing up, Eban's eyes narrowed as he saw Denver standing in front of him. "Yes. What do you want, Denver?"

"I was hoping to talk to you a minute."

"Oh?"

Denver expelled a soft breath. It was obvious to him that trying to win over Sierra's brother was going to be an uphill battle.

"Yeah." Denver spoke softly. "I realized that even though I apologized to Sierra, I never did apologize to you. So, I wanted to say that I am truly sorry for how I abandoned your sister on what was supposed to be our wedding day years ago."

"Sorry huh. And that's going to fix it, just like that?" Eban's blue eyes, so like Sierra's, glittered with pent up anger.

"No, I don't suppose it will fix it. But, all I can say is I'm doing my best to right past wrongs. And I hope someday you can forgive me."

The silence grew tight with tension.

"Maybe. I'll admit that my sister seems to be happier with you now than she ever was with Stuart. But, that doesn't make the past disappear, Denver."

"I know. That's what I'm working on fixing."

"What about your son, Cody? I've done my best to be a father figure in his life for the past six years, when you were no where to be found. What are you doing about that?"

Denver sobered. "Yeah. I do regret not being there when Cody was born and to help Sierra raise him. I didn't even know I had a son until I arrived back in town."

"It's my own fault for not knowing, because I didn't reply to Sierra's letter six years ago." Denver sighed and ran a shaky hand through his hair. "But, I've been getting to know Cody. He's a great boy any father would be proud of."

"You're right about that." Eban nodded and wiped his oily hands on a dry cloth as he studied him. "At least you're taking a step in the right direction by getting to know your son and righting old wrongs, I'll say that at least."

Denver nodded, realizing that was probably a high compliment coming from Sierra's brother. "Thanks. I'll keep trying."

"But, I'm warning you. Don't hurt my sister again Denver because you won't like the consequences." Eban shot him a cold look.

"Duly noted. I promise to do everything I can not to cause Sierra anymore pain, Eban." Denver nodded and turned to walk away, when loud barks were heard outside of the garage.

"That's strange. Sounded like a dog, but we don't have a dog." Eban hurried behind him to look outside.

Denver turned and grinned, pointing to his truck. A

cute brown, black and white puppy pushed his nose up against the window of Denver's truck.

"I'm giving Cody a puppy as an early Christmas gift."

Eban nodded smiling. "Well, I think Cody will love it. He's been asking for a dog for a long time. But, I'm not sure about Sierra. She hasn't been big on surprises ever since my parent's accident years ago."

A sobering frown fell on Denver. "I understand. I've actually been doing some digging into the accident. When Sierra explained what happened years ago, something didn't seem to add up."

"Sierra won't like you digging around. But, I'm all for it. If there is anything the police missed, I want to know about it." Eban's words rang with determination.

"So you don't mind if my Private Investigator comes to take a look at the car that was used in the accident?" Denver remembered that Jake Davis his investigator had been asking yesterday to search the car for clues.

"I don't mind at all. Granddad tied a large tarp over the car twenty years ago, and it hasn't been touched since. It's right over there." Eban pointed to the covered up vehicle in the garage parked on the other side of his truck. "Sierra doesn't like to be reminded of the accident, so you might have trouble convincing her."

"I'll do my best." Denver nodded and then reached into the truck to grab the puppy.

He waved at a smiling Eban and walked toward the ranch house. He put the long leash on the puppy and tied it to the front of the deck, so that he wouldn't run away.

As soon as he knocked on the door, Sierra answered.

"Hey beautiful."

A tremulous smile formed on Sierra's mouth. He wanted to pull her into his arms and kiss those sweet lips, but he heard feet bouncing on the floor behind her.

"I came to give our son a surprise. It's an early Christmas gift."

"You're giving Cody a surprise Christmas gift?" Sierra looked past Denver, her blue eyes widening at the sight of the small fluffy puppy. "Oh my. Denver, I don't know if this is such a good idea…"

Cody appeared at her side and seeing Denver threw his little arms around his waist. "Denver you're here. I'm glad."

A warm glow flowed through Denver at his son's hug. Wrapping his arms around his son, he sighed happily. "Hey buddy."

Man, he could really get used to this feeling of contentment, joy and belonging.

All of a sudden his thoughts were interrupted by loud barks.

Cody pulled himself away from his dad's arms and turned to see the puppy. His green eyes grew wide. "You brought a puppy. Can I pet him?"

"Of course, son." Denver grinned at Cody's excitement. He looked over at Sierra his eyes seeking her approval to give their son this unexpected gift. She sighed and nodded, her smile warm.

Cody ran over to the puppy, scratching behind his ears and resting his boyish face against the dogs neck. The dog began licking his cheek.

Cody giggled.

"Ah… he's so nice. Is this your dog, Denver?"

"Actually, this puppy is yours Cody. This dog is an early Christmas present just for you."

A cry of joy broke from his son's lips. "You're giving me, my very own puppy?"

"Yep." Denver grinned as Cody gave him another big hug.

"Thank you so much. You're the best Dad ever." His son's small arms squeezed his waist and lingered. Denver leaned over and kissed the top of his son's head, so pleased to hear his son call him Dad. "Did you hear that Mom? Dad gave me my very own dog." His son looked over at Sierra who chuckled at her son's enthusiasm.

"That is exciting, Cody. What are you going to name him?" Sierra walked down the deck steps and went down on her knees to put the new puppy.

Cody followed, looking unsure as he thought about. "I'll call him Cocoa. He has lots of brown fur that looks like chocolate. And I like chocolate, so I think that's a good name for him."

"That's a great name, son." Sierra kissed his cheek before standing to her feet.

Sierra blue eyes studied him, contemplative gleam shone in them and she smiled. He gloried briefly in their shared moment of joy with their son.

He found he was longing for more of those moments of shared joy with Sierra.

More than anything, he wanted to have that second chance for them to be a family. He wanted that second chance for happiness. He wanted that second chance for love.

HER SON WAS SO happy with his new puppy that she just let him play. But, she needed to talk to Denver.

"Walk with me for a little while?" She turned towards Denver. He nodded and began to walk beside her.

"I don't usually like surprises, but judging by the big grin on our son's face, giving him a puppy as a gift was a good one. Thank you for doing that."

She watched the play of emotions on Denver's face. "I shouldn't have unexpectedly sprung the dog on you. I should have asked if that was okay with you first."

"Thanks. I appreciate you saying that. But, I believe you just made our son happy for today and for months or even years to come." She chuckled and turned for a minute watching Cody rolling on the ground with his new dog.

Denver watched the two of them and grinned. "Looks that way."

They walked in silence for a little longer before she spoke again. "I really need to tell you about some problems I'm having with at the coffee shop. And maybe you can give me some ideas on how I should tackle this problem."

"Sure. Tell me what's up?"

Sierra told Denver everything she had shared with Mrs. Jenkins about Aunt Serena's concerns that the profit margins for the coffee shop were very low. "I saw the strangest thing as I was leaving Mrs. Jenkins house today."

She paused for a moment. "Stuart drove up to my aunt's house and it looked like the two of them were having a cozy chat. I think it's possible that Stuart is Aunt Serena's accountant. Then the thought occurred to me that perhaps he's found some way to get back at me for ending our engagement."

Denver nodded and looked beyond them at the clear blue sky, deep in thought. "Well, if Stuart was doing something underhanded with the way he keeps records for your business account, that's illegal. He could get into a lot of trouble doing that."

Denver went on. "However, one way we could quietly see what's going on, is to get Jake to do some investigating. I'm sure it wouldn't take him long to look into it."

"You would do that?"

"Sierra, I'm here to help you, in whatever way I can. I hope you can believe that."

"I do. Thanks Denver." Sierra sighed with relief. "I feel better knowing that someone will look into it. It frustrates me that my aunt thinks I would try to do something to hinder the profit of our business."

Denver shook his head in disbelief. "Well, if she thinks that, then she doesn't know your character very well. I don't know anyone who works harder, has more integrity or cares more about her business or people than you."

"I appreciate you saying that, Denver." Sierra swallowed back emotion at his praise. "Not everyone would agree with you, but I appreciate it all the same."

"Well if they don't agree, it's because either they don't know you, or they have some ill will against you."

Sierra nodded. "Thanks."

Denver grabbed her hand and squeezed her smaller

one gently. "I'll contact Jake and we will get to the bottom of this, I promise."

"I appreciate that."

He nodded. "Of course." He hesitated a moment before he continued. "Since we're on the topic of Jake and his investigative skills, I wanted to ask if you would be okay if he stopped by the farm to look at the car from the accident?"

A melancholy frown flitted across her features as she was reminded of how her parents died. She didn't like the constant reminders about it.

"I guess. But if Jake doesn't find anything and you're satisfied, can we agree that we will let the matter rest?" Her blue eyes were wide and imploring.

"Yes, of course." Denver put one arm around her waist, pulling her close to his side. She felt him kiss the top of her head and she melted into his embrace.

They walked in peaceful silence for a moment, before Denver whispered. "Now let's talk about something cheerful. Tell me, have you started reading your mother's journals yet?"

Sierra smiled thinking on what she'd read so far. "Yes. I've been reading my mother's journals for the past few days and I've managed to read through quite a few of her stories."

"Go on, I'd like to hear this." His soothing voice probed further.

"Okay." Sierra found her mother's stories interesting and didn't mind sharing them. "Well, my mom starts the journal by saying, that she hopes her children and grandchildren would read the stories she writes in hopes that they will understand their families history. But, she also hopes that readers will learn the importance of forgiveness."

Peering over at Denver, she could see he was listening intently so she continued. "My mom started by writing the story of her parents. She said her father Arthur Jeffries, was always a man on the lookout for the next better opportunity."

"He started out life as a hard worker and worked to become manager of a company. During this time he met and married his first wife Marion. They were only married for five years before Marion died of heart failure. Her daughter Serena was only two years old at the time."

Sierra took a breath and continued the story. "My mother wrote that it was only six months after the death of Arthur Jeffries first wife, that he met Sophia Anderson."

"My mom wrote that her father was always looking for his calculated next move and it would prove to be helpful that he met and later married Sophia Anderson. She was one six children born to Edward Anderson, the founder of Anderson Beauty and Cosmetics."

"Your grandfather married into a wealthy family. Anderson Cosmetics is known internationally." Denver let out a low whistle.

"Yes, it's hard to believe isn't it?"

Sierra continued with the story. "Arthur Jeffries didn't like it that Sophia's father insisted that certain conditions be met before he could marry his daughter. Edward Anderson insisted that a large amount of money be set aside in a trust for each of their children."

"I guess Edward Anderson also insisted that the estate

and the cabin by the lake, which Sophia loved, be placed only in Sophia's name. That was the only way he would agree to the marriage. So Arthur Jeffries agreed."

"Mom wrote in her journal that she remembered hearing arguments about money by the time she was five and six years of age. By the time they were married for only seven years, Arthur Jeffries had lost or gambled away most of the money from their marriage."

Denver shook his head.

"Mom remembered the one time during a big argument her father said I am in deep debt. We have to sell the estate or the cabin by the lake. Her mother told him, I can't do that and I won't. My father insisted that I hold onto it. Then, her father asked her mother, what am I going to do? Her mother replied he needed to stop gambling and get an honest job."

"Her father stomped out of the house and went a little wild after that — drinking and chasing after women. She writes that her mother could smell women's perfume and see strange lipstick on his clothes when he came home after many late nights."

Sierra sighed heavily. "My mom writes that her and her stepsister had many arguments during their childhood and teen years. Serena insisted that Amelia got the most of their father and mother's attention. And usually found petty ways to get back at her, like spreading rumors about her that weren't true or doing her best to take Amelia's boyfriends away." Sierra sighed.

"Then, my mom writes that her mother cried a lot and later she found out that's when a long affair had begun between Arthur Jeffries and another woman. I can't remember her name just now. It's in the journal." Reading about the story of her grandparents and parents chaotic lives, was incredible.

Denver walked beside her in silence, his thoughts seemed far away.

"That's as far as I've read in the journals so far. I'm sad that my mom and aunt Serena didn't really get along."

"Yeah, that is sad." Denver shook his head. "As you read more, I'd like to hear it. It's a sad and moving story."

"It is. I still can't believe all that drama is part of my history."

"Sometimes our parent's or grandparent's history can really surprise us. I know that first hand."

"I know you do. I'm sorry Denver." She tucked her hand in his.

Of course sharing her mother's journals would be a reminder of the rough start Denver had when his dad left and his mom died when he was just a young child.

"It's all right. Each of us had experienced difficulties at some time or other in our families. I'm glad I can help be there for you as you're finding more details about your family." He put his arm around her waist.

Pulling her into a close embrace, he whispered. "I just want to be there for you, no matter what you're going through."

Tears moistened her eyes and she swallowed quickly. "Thank you Denver. That means the world to me."

CHAPTER TWELVE

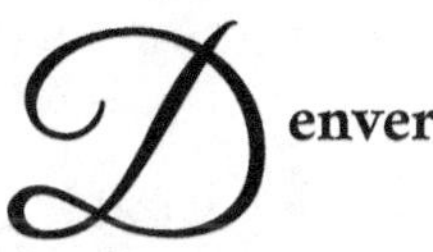enver

A PERSISTENT BUZZ jerked Denver out of a deep sleep.

Fumbling in the dark he reached across to the night-stand and grabbed his phone.

"Denver here." He pushed himself up in bed and rubbed his eyes. Looking at the time on his phone, he realized he'd slept in.

He wondered who was calling. Only family members and a very select group of people important in his life had his private number.

"Morning Denver. It's Jake Davis."

He braced himself at the sound of his Private Investigator's voice. There could only be a few reasons Jake was calling this morning.

"Any news?"

"Yes on a couple of fronts actually." In a cool, detached voice, Jake described what he'd discovered. "I was able to search documents in Stuart Gardiner's office."

"From our investigation, we have reason to believe Stuart has been taking most of the profits from the coffee shop and making multiple small deposits, spreading them into different accounts."

Jake paused for a moment before continuing. "We don't have the proof we need yet. We're still searching where the money has gone. I've contacted the police and they are looking into it now. But, if they confirm what I suspect from the documents I've given them, the police will be arresting him soon."

Denver sighed, glad that the day of reckoning wouldn't be postponed forever. "So, it seems Sierra was right about her former fiancé. He figured out a way to get his revenge."

"I think so. We'll know more from the police either today or tomorrow."

"I look forward to it." Denver breathed a sigh of relief. "Any updates on the vehicle from the car accident?"

"Yes. I had an expert mechanic inspect the vehicle who specializes in automobile sabotage. When he realized the car was an antique made in the 1930s, he searched the brake line and found that it had been cut."

Jake continued. "He explained that back in the 1920s and 1930s cars had the brakes on all four wheels connected to the same reservoir. If there was a leak anywhere in the system, eventually all the brake fluid would leak out until you had no brakes at all."

"So it looks like someone tampered with the car after all."

"That's what it looks like. So now we are searching for the name of the teenager found on Baxter's farm twenty years ago." He paused for a moment before adding. "And of course we are searching for any other information that we may have missed."

Denver sighed, running a hand through his hair. "So Sierra's parents' car accident wasn't really an accident after all."

"That's what it looks like. We'll know more after the police do another search."

"Well, I'm glad you're searching for that teenager from twenty years ago. I'll feel better once we have all the loose ends tied up and the people who are responsible for these crimes are in custody. They have hurt too many people already."

Denver's tone of voice was cool and unyielding. "Thanks again for all the hard work and time you've put into this investigation, Jake."

"Oh don't worry, my hard work will be reflected on my bill."

Denver chuckled. "I'm sure it will. Talk to you later."

He hung up the phone and sat there for a moment, thinking of all the emotional pain and heartache Sierra and the rest of the Baxter family had already been through because of whoever was responsible for these crimes.

As for Stuart, Denver was convinced the police would discover that he was money laundering from Sierra and her aunt's coffee business.

It couldn't happen soon enough as far as he was concerned.

Denver hurried to get dressed, thinking of the busy day ahead.

Tonight was the culmination of the Christmas Fair.

There would be a Christmas potluck and of course the theme would be The Twelve Days of Christmas.

He would pick up Sierra and Cody as planned. But, he decided he wouldn't tell Sierra about what he learned about Stuart or about the car accident just yet.

He wanted them to be able to enjoy this night, without any worries.

Sierra had asked if Cody should stay home with Grams since he would likely be tired out early in the evening.

Denver convinced her that their son should come with them. He could see his friends and have fun. He promised he would watch out for him and see to it that Cody was safe.

So, Sierra had agreed.

Their small town of Refuge Mountain had a unique way of creating events for the whole town that made everyone feel like they were part of a big family.

This event would be no different with the potluck and the sleigh rides and hayrides afterwards.

It would be fun.

Pulling a small box out of his pocket, he opened it up and stared for a moment at the marquis style diamond that twinkled in the sun's reflection.

Most of all Denver hoped that it would be an evening that both he and Sierra would remember.

SIERRA CLUNG to Denver's arm as they walked through the double doors of the community center.

Cody ran ahead of them when he saw his best friends Noah and Caleb.

Nervously, her hands fisted the soft red velvet cocktail length dress she wore. Turning her head she basked in the warmth of Denver's warm smile.

He looked especially handsome tonight. The dark forest green sports jacket he wore only emphasized his broad shoulders and vivid green eyes.

"So what's the verdict? Will I do?"

Her breath quickened and her cheeks became warm at his teasing words.

"As usual, you look very handsome." The words rushed out of her mouth.

He put one arm around her waist and leaning his mouth next to her ear he whispered. "And you are incredibly beautiful. I'm the luckiest man here tonight."

Sierra blushed at his compliment. Lately, it seemed he was always saying the most wonderful things to her.

She was about to reply when someone called her name. "Sounds like someone is eager to talk to you. I'll go join my brothers." Denver whispered and kissed her cheek, before walking away.

"Sierra, I'm glad you're here." Abby walked towards her wearing a blue dress that suited her auburn hair.

"I am. I love that blue dress on you." Sierra smiled at her friend. "I see your boys Joey and Tony have already found friends to hang with. My son seems to have attached himself to Noah and Caleb. I'm sure he's already excited about the hayride afterwards."

"Yeah. Our kids will have fun. I believe Wyatt expects me to stay indoors tonight. He's incredibly protective now that I'm pregnant." Abby sighed, placing one hand over the bulge on her belly.

"Well, he's a father who is protective of his family. I think that's normal." Lately, Sierra had experienced more of that same protectiveness from Denver. She liked it that he wanted to protect both her and Cody.

"It is normal." They walked together toward the drink table. Sierra poured drinks for both of them. "How have you been feeling?"

Abby smiled softly. "I've had the occasional morning sickness. Other than that I'm doing great. Yesterday I felt the fluttering of the baby for the first time. Wyatt is as excited as I am."

Sierra grinned. "I can tell. I'm so happy for you both, it really is wonderful to experience the miracle of a new baby."

"It is." Abby leaned closer and spoke in a half whisper. "I hope you and Denver marry so we can truly be sisters."

Sierra felt a rush of happiness at that thought. Reminders of past hurt and pain still tried to plant doubt and fear in her mind at getting closer to Denver. But, he had really won her over.

"I do too." She whispered back, a wistful look in her eyes.

Abby's eyes sparkled and she laughed gently. "It'll happen, my friend."

On the inside Sierra questioned that statement. Would it really happen for her and Denver? She hoped so.

One of Abby's boys needed her attention and her friend hurried away. Sierra sipped at her drink as she pondered her friend's words.

Looking around the crowded community center, she spotted Denver. Beside him stood a tall slender woman with long dark brown hair, who stood close. As he talked to her, she continued to lean closer.

Sierra felt a possessive jealousy surface from deep inside.

Who was that woman? And why was Denver standing so close to her whispering in her ear?

Her lips thinned in irritation. She wanted to march over there and demand to know who she was, but of course she wasn't about to make a scene. Instead she gulped back her drink and turned to fill up her small cup for another.

Aunt Serena came to stand by her side. Her dark eyes glittered a little as she stared at her. "Hello niece. You look like your mother, all dressed up like that."

"Thank you Aunt Serena. I've always wanted to be just like my mom." Sierra sighed thinking of the journals she'd been reading.

"Hmm. Your mother wasn't perfect you know, even though she was beautiful." Her aunt looked at the juice in her cup for a moment, her voice sounding faraway before she turned back to Sierra. "I hope you have a wonderful evening my dear. You've earned it."

Sierra wondered at her aunt's words, they sounded

strange. But she shrugged it off and took a sip of her drink.

Her friend Sarah walked toward her.

"Sarah. What a nice surprise." Sierra forced a smile, trying to get a grip of the irritation she was feeling. She pulled Sarah into a warm hug. "Is your grandfather here with you?"

"He's just talking with Sheriff Hank Turnbull." A tiny furrow of worry appeared between Sarah's brows. "I think he's disturbed by our neighbor who continues to pester Granddad about buying his land and making me his wife. I think he's trying to get the Sheriff's legal opinion on it."

"Your neighbor can't force you to be his wife." The whole idea was ridiculous and somewhat disturbing to Sierra.

"Aye, it's not legal, that's true enough. But our brute neighbor really is a force to be reckoned with and has this strange notion that my Granddad offered me to him, saying that I would be his wife. Which is something Granddad didn't agree to, but it's stuck in his craw anyways." Sarah's Scottish brogue became more pronounced when she was upset about something.

"Well there must be some way to stop your neighbor. Either that, or hurry and marry someone else."

Sierra meant it as a joke, but Sarah nodded solemnly, as her eyes strayed to her Grandfather. "That's funny, that's what Granddad said as we came down from the mountain and into town yesterday."

"He told me, Sarah we will find a legal way from the Sheriff to get ourselves out of this problem with our neighbor or I'll find the quickest way to marry you to a man we both like and respect." Sarah bit her lip as she looked over at her Granddad. "What worries me is I know my Granddad means it."

Sierra sighed heavily. "I'm sorry for the trouble you're in. If there's anything I can do to help?"

Sarah's eyes turned misty. "Thank you for offering to help. But, I don't think there's anything you can do. I think Granddad is just worried because he's been sick this past year and is worried that he doesn't have much time left on this earth. He's told me he wants to see me married and settled before he dies."

"Your grandfather is just concerned about you, I'm sure." Sierra turned to see Sarah's grandfather Angus MacDonald in a spirited conversation with Sheriff Turnbull.

Dakota Callahan had joined the two men and talked to Angus, which seemed to calm the older man down some. Dakota looked over at Sierra and then turned to look at Sarah, his dark gaze piercing and intense as he watched her.

Sierra turned back to look at Sarah, not missing the roses that blossomed in her cheeks. At that moment, Sierra wondered if Sarah didn't already have a man in mind she was interested in marrying.

"Things will turn out for the best, Sarah. I have great faith in your grandfather and in you to make the wisest of decisions." Sierra squeezed her friend's hand gently.

"Thanks Sierra. That means a lot." Sarah spoke softly, a hopeful glint in her eyes.

Mrs. Moore began speaking from the microphone at the front of the large community center.

"Please, find your seats everyone." Mrs. Moore pulled out a piece of paper that she began reading from.

"Talk to you later." Sierra smiled at Sarah and waved goodbye before she looked for her son. She found him standing next to Denver.

Sierra saw the woman in the green dress still beside him. Walking up to Denver she forced a smile. "I see you have a friend with you Denver. I'd love an introduction."

Sierra forced a smile and noticed the woman's brown eyes look over her critically.

"Sierra Baxter, this is Jade Barlow, a friend from Nashville. She's here for a short visit to our small town." Denver moved so he stood closer to Sierra, placing a hand on the small of her back.

"Yes. I caught one of your live shows on television and wanted to see if this small town was as adorable in real life as it's reported to be on television." Jade's tone of voice dripped with disdain.

"And what did you decide?" She masked her inner turmoil with a deceptive calmness.

"Well it is cute, but it lacks sophistication and culture. I did my master's degree in Architectural Design and I can see many buildings along Main Street that could use a re-do to better fit with the look and feel of this small town." Jade's words were cool and aloof. "What did you study in college, Sierra?"

Sierra struggled with insecurity as she stood face to face with this beautiful woman. She never had a chance to go to college. In fact, the only reason she was able to receive her High School diploma was from spending hours in the evenings taking courses after Cody was born.

"I didn't go to college." A glimmer of satisfaction appeared in Jade's brown eyes. Sierra tried not to be cowed by insecurity as she continued. "I understand what you're saying about the building designs on Main Street. But, I think something to consider is that maybe the unique look of each of those buildings might be part of their small town charm."

"Based on my several years of education and experience, I'd have to say I don't agree."

Sierra smiled. "I guess that's the beautiful thing about art. Everyone is welcome to share their own ideas and opinions on it."

His hand squeezed against her waist. "It looks like it's time to sit down at our tables. We'll talk with you later, Jade."

Denver pulled her to his side and they walked toward the table where his mother was seated along with his brothers and Abby and their two boys.

Sierra whispered. "Just out of curiosity, is Jade one of your old girlfriends?"

He sighed. "Yeah. I didn't expect her to show up here. She just showed up expectedly. The real problem, is that she doesn't seem to understand when I tell her I don't want to see her anymore."

"Hmm. Maybe you're not convincing enough."

"Well beautiful, I could kiss you right here and now and maybe that would finally convince her."

"Denver, stop teasing." Sierra giggled.

"Who's teasing? I'm deadly serious." Denver's green eyes glittered dangerously and he leaned closer, staring at her lips.

Sierra stepped a little away from him. "Denver Callahan. We are in a room full of people, you can't kiss me in front of everyone."

"Relax. If you say so, I won't kiss you now." He whispered against her hair next to her ear. "But, I will take a rain check for later this evening."

A rush of pink stained her cheeks as she sat down at the table beside Cody and next to Mrs. Callahan and the rest of their family.

Sierra took a sip of water, trying to stop the surge of mixed emotions going through her.

Mrs. Moore was talking a little more explaining about the evening, when she stopped.

"Father Tim will say a blessing over our meal and then we'll line up by the tables to the right to get our food. Father Tim?" Mrs. Moore handed the microphone over to the Father.

"It's a pleasure each year to join you all in celebrating Christmas, the season of miracles, peace and love. I pray a special blessing rests on you and your families tonight and throughout this Christmas season." Father Tim continued by praying a blessing over the food.

After the blessing, each of the folks from town formed a line along a side table that was filled with food.

Everyone filled their plates and returned to their tables to eat and enjoy conversation. When they finished eating Mrs. Moore returned to stand at the podium.

"As you all know these past three weeks we've celebrated our annual Christmas Fair. You can see the theme on the banner behind me, The Twelve Days of Christmas.

Many of you will have seen the theme around town on the doors of many small businesses."

"And you might have also had a chance to watch the live show with Denver Callahan and Sierra Baxter each morning." Folks from town started clapping as Mrs. Moore nodded in their direction.

"We wanted to honor everyone who contributed to our annual Christmas Fair with this plaque of recognition. Each of you can hang it on your wall, as a fond reminder of how you helped contribute to our small town of Refuge Mountain's Christmas tradition."

Everyone clapped as folks were handed their commemorative wood tablet.

"This year has been a resounding success. We have doubled the viewership of our town's morning television show with our annual Christmas Fair. And the businesses around our small town have boomed. I believe in many ways it's thanks to Denver and Sierra and their team's hard work." Mrs. Moore's expression brightened as her gaze fell on Denver and Sierra again.

Mrs. Moore continued. "If I may speak for everyone here, I don't mind saying we hope the two of you will consider co-hosting next year's Christmas Fair."

"Hear, hear." Jed Burnside from Burnside Art Gallery spoke loudly and a couple of other folks echoed the sentiment.

Sierra blushed with the praise and turned to Denver.

"We'll consider it. Thanks for your confidence in us." Denver spoke loudly enough for everyone to hear.

Sierra was caught up in the enthusiasm until she

happened to glance at Jade Barlow. The hostile glare that was sent her way, made her shiver just a little.

Sierra hoped Denver's girlfriend would leave town as soon as possible. She really didn't want to have to deal with more things or people causing heartache in her life.

Soon, Mrs. Moore returned to the microphone.

"Our volunteers will hand out dessert and coffee and after that, whoever wants to go on a sleigh ride or hay ride, meet at the front doors. We'll wind up tonight's event with some fun for everyone."

Sierra grinned at the excitement from the children, especially her own son.

"You'll need to wait until after everyone has had time to eat dessert, then

"I need to go to the washroom. Be right back." Sierra whispered to Denver.

"Hurry back." Denver squeezed her hand and she hurried to the far end of the main room. After she began to walk back, Stuart Gardiner suddenly stepped in front of her.

"Sierra, you look beautiful as usual tonight." She stood motionless at the cold disdain in her former fiancé's tone of voice.

"Stuart. Was there something you wanted?"

"Now, Sierra you sound irritated. Is that anyway to talk to the man you planned to marry?" His syrupy sweet tone was enough to irritate her.

"I ended our engagement, remember?"

"Ah yes. In my office, I remember now." Stuart's tone suddenly became chilly. "And speaking of my office and the valuable work I do there, I want to ask you: Do you have any idea about who searched through my important documents?"

Sierra sighed in exasperation. "No. Why would I know anything about any documents you keep?"

At her quick answer, Stuart stammered and his eyes narrowed studying hers. "No specific reason. Except that your aunt told me she informed you that your coffee business is bleeding almost all your profit dollars."

"Wait a minute." Sierra's tone hardened. "You wouldn't know about any of those details unless you are my Aunt Serena's accountant. Are you?"

"I am."

Sierra questioned him further. "Does that mean you are also responsible for handling the books for the coffee shop?"

"Yes. And let me tell you, you really need to learn how to make a profit or you're going to end up losing the business completely." His taunting irritated her.

Sierra pushed her shoulders back. "But, if someone was doing something to try to force me out of business, that might be a reason my business would look on paper, that I wasn't making a profit. For example, if someone wanted revenge that might be a tactic they'd try right?" Sierra lowered her voice, the steely edge in her tone of voice being purposefully mysterious.

Stuart's face paled and the silence between them grew tight with tension.

His laugh sounded forced. "You don't know what you're talking about. Have a nice evening, Sierra."

A pulsing knot started in her belly and worked its way up. She wanted to know what he was up to.

She really hoped Denver would talk to his private investigator. They really needed some answers and soon.

Forcing a light smile on her face, she hurried back to their table and sat down between Cody and Denver.

"Looks like most folks have finished eating. It's time for the hayride, right Cody?" Denver grinned.

Sierra was happy Cody was having fun with his friends.

"Yay. I'm excited." Cody jumped to his feet.

Joey and Tony did the same. As the children and a few adults began to line up at the front door, Cody and his cousins turned to go.

"Cody, wait a minute." Sierra whispered and double checked that his coat, gloves and wool hat were firmly in place. She turned to look at Denver. "Are you going with him on the hayride?"

"I think he'll be fine Sierra, as long as he sticks close to Joey and Tony and his friends Noah and Caleb. There's also a bunch of adults going with them too. I really think they'll be fine." Denver smiled with confidence.

Sierra expelled a breath. "You're right, I'm being an overprotective mom again." Turning to Cody she whispered. "Stick close to Joey and Tony and have fun. We will be here waiting when you get back, okay?"

"Okay mom. I love you."

"And I love you, little bean."

After kissing him on the cheek, she waved him off as all the children hurried out of the community center to the back of the wagon filled with hay.

Sierra stood by the door and waved as the children left the yard. Two horses pulled the wagon filled with hay and children. Excited laughter filled the air and Sierra turned to Denver with a smile.

"This is fun for him." Sierra couldn't stop the anxious knot in her belly. "I can't help but feel a little worried. He's my little boy and has hardly been out of my sight, except to be with Grams or Eban."

"I understand. Would it help if we waited for him outside by the campfire? That way Cody will see us as soon as they return."

"Yes. That I'd feel better if we did that."

Denver slipped his hand on her waist, pulling her gently to his side. They walked together to the large campfire someone had built outside.

Sierra moved restlessly and looked around. There weren't that many folks who stayed for the hayride, but she guessed the older folks probably wanted to get home.

The hayride was more for the children anyway.

She looked around for Aunt Serena or Stuart but didn't see either of them. And Jade Barlow was nowhere to be found either.

Well, it was just as well.

It seemed like it took forever until Sierra spotted the horses turning the corner coming back from the hayride.

They were riding in quite fast, she hoped they would be able to stop okay.

Denver turned with her to watch the kids tumble off the hay wagon when it finally came to a stop.

Sierra looked for Cody, but couldn't see his grinning face anywhere. He must be on the other side of the wagon, she supposed.

All of a sudden, Joey and Tony came running towards her, stopping in front of her and Denver.

"You won't believe it. Cody is missing. None of us are sure what happened, but one minute he was sitting between Tony and me and the next minute I turned, Cody had disappeared."

Sierra choked back a cry, frightened and filled with dread.

"What do you mean my son is gone? How could he simply have gone missing? What happened?" A tight knot formed in her belly and her eyes widened as she looked from Joey to Denver.

Denver held her close. "We will find him, I promise Sierra. Now Joey, tell us one more time what happened. Sheriff Turnbull is here and he needs to hear what happened."

Joey repeated what he had told Sierra and added that he didn't know how Cody could have simply disappeared without someone seeing him.

Sheriff Turnbull spoke. "We will find your son, Sierra. I promise you, I will find whoever did this, and bring your son back."

The Sheriff moved away, issuing orders to the people to stay put, so he could question every person there.

In the distance, Sierra could hear people mobilizing around her but all she felt was a numb kind of shock overtake her senses.

Her little boy was gone. Where was he? Who would have taken him and why?

She began to shake as fearful images built in her imagination of what was happening with her son.

Denver's arms wrapped around her and he held her close in his strong arms. "We will find our son, Sierra. I don't care what it takes, we will bring our son home." His tone was hard as steel and just as determined.

Hearing his words, tears slowly found their way down her cheeks, silently flowing faster until deep sobs racked her insides.

Despite Denver's words, she doubted. Perhaps just like she lost her parents years ago, so to her son was gone. Would she never hold him in her arms again?

CHAPTER THIRTEEN

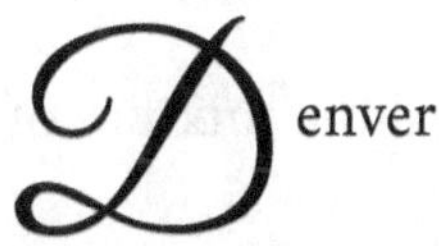enver

LOUD RINGING TONES continued to sound at the other end of the phone line.

Denver paced waiting for his brother to pick up on the other end.

He glanced over at Sierra, who sat huddled with a blanket around her shoulders, near the wood stove in the community center kitchen.

Sitting nearby was her brother Eban and her friend Sarah.

They were talking in hushed tones, doing their best to give Sierra the comfort and support she needed.

A glazed look of despair had wrapped itself around her face since learning her son was missing last night.

It was now dawn and she still hadn't slept. Neither of them had.

Fear had been their constant companion throughout the night.

His thoughts were interrupted when he heard his brother's voice.

"Dakota here." Denver sighed in relief as he finally answered. There was a groggy sound to his voice. "Sorry to wake you up, man. But, I need your help."

"Sure. What's up?"

Denver pushed back the pain in his heart, to reply in even tones. "My son went missing late last night."

"What?"

He felt strangely comforted as he heard the mixture of surprise and anger in Dakota's voice.

"Yes, Sierra and I are both stunned that our son just disappeared."

Denver explained what they knew up to this point. "And so Sheriff Turnbull and much of the police force of Refuge Mountain have been searching the town. Even many of the folks from town have volunteered to search for him. They've been walking on foot throughout the night, searching the entire town calling out Cody's name. But they haven't found my son anywhere."

Denver spoke in a low, tormented voice. "But, I know you have had great success finding people when you were hired by the FBI to track and find missing persons. That's why I called you, Dakota. I'm asking for your help to find my son."

"Of course I'll help, Denver. I will do everything in my

power to help you find Cody. Hang tight, I'll be there soon."

Denver sighed feeling more at ease now that he knew Dakota would be helping with the search. His brother had an uncanny skill for tracking animals or people. In every case he'd been hired to solve with the FBI, he had found the missing people quickly.

Walking over to where Sierra was seated by her friends and sat down across from her. "Dakota is coming to help with the search for Cody."

Her head was bowed, her body slumped under the blanket in despair. Slowly she looked up at him and nodded silently, her face bleak with sorrow.

The pain in his heart became a sick and fiery gnawing at seeing the woman he loved filled with so much heartache.

Her brother and friend sat and stood nearby and he really needed to talk to Sierra without any listening ears.

"Eban and Sarah, if you could give us a moment, I'd like to talk to Sierra alone."

As soon as the two friends left, Denver sat beside Sierra. Placing his arm gently around her shoulders, he pulled her close.

"We will find our son, sweetheart."

Sierra turned to him, her voice filled with agony. "How do you know that? We don't have any idea where he could've gone or who has him."

"Yes those are the facts right now. But I know we'll find Cody, simply because I will not give up until I do." A new determination rose up inside him as he realized the depth of his determination to do just that.

She nodded. "I'm glad Denver, I really am. It just seems so hopeless." Her hands twisted the blanket and trembled slightly.

"We have so many people helping in this search. It's not hopeless." Denver tried to reassure her.

"I know." Sierra nodded. "I keep thinking back to what happened last night. We should never have let him go by himself — without one of his parents — on that hayride. Or maybe we should have said no when he asked us to go in the first place."

"Maybe." Denver sighed heavily. "I realize I encouraged Cody to go on the hayride more than you did. I'm sorry if I did the wrong thing by doing that. But, I don't think it will help us to focus on everything that went wrong. Instead, we should be putting all our energy into figuring out how to find our son."

Tears glistened on her pale face and she nodded. "You're right. We should be focused on finding Cody right now." Hurriedly, she wiped tears away. "So what do we need to do next?"

Denver kissed the top of her head and spoke softly. "We are waiting for Sheriff Turnbull to return and for Dakota to get here. Then we'll be able to plan our next steps."

"All right."

The ringing tone of Denver's phone interrupted them at that moment. He looked down to see Jake Davis' name on his screen.

"I need to take this. I'll be back in a minute." She nodded and Denver walked a distance away to talk to his private investigator.

"What's up Jake?"

"So, we finally learned the name of the teenager who was on Baxter's farm the morning of the day the car accident happened twenty years ago."

"Who was it?"

"His name is Art Thompson. The police have brought him to the police station for questioning."

"That's good. Let me know if you learn anything else."

"Will do, Denver. Later."

Denver hung up the phone just as his brother walked into the community center.

"Dakota, thanks for coming." Denver gave his brother a quick hug, feeling relief at having his brother's support. "We need all the help we can get. And I'm grateful."

"You're welcome."

Denver heard the door open again and in walked Sheriff Turnbull along with a couple of his officers.

The Sheriff walked over to Denver, lifting his officer's hat he ran a hand through his grey hair before placing the service hat back on his head. "So far, we haven't found any clues as to Cody's whereabouts. We've looked all around the town — including many volunteers who have walked the entire town on foot. Any other places where we should look?"

Denver thought for a moment. "Lately Stuart Gardiner — Sierra's former fiancé — has been creating a little trouble with accounting details for Sierra and her aunt's coffee business. Do you think we should search Stuart's place?"

"I'll get someone on it." The Sheriff called another officer on his two-way radio to go search the house.

Dakota looked over to where Sierra was. "I think a great place to find more answers is to ask Sierra some questions."

Sheriff Turnbull returned and nodded. "That's a good idea." He walked beside Dakota across the room towards Sierra. "You used to work for the FBI finding missing persons didn't you?"

"Yeah. I learned a thing or two that should hopefully help us find Cody.

"That's great." Sheriff and his officers stood to the side while Dakota sat across from Sierra.

Denver sat beside her and squeezed her hand. "Dakota has a few questions to ask that will help him search for our son."

"Okay." Sierra shrugged in resignation. Denver sensed she was feeling hopeless that Cody would be found.

He held her hand, in an effort to offer what comfort he could

Dakota began. "I need to ask questions. Take your time to answer them. Some of the questions won't be easy, which is why it's important to remember we all want the same thing. To find Cody."

Sierra sighed and nodded. "First of all have there been any specific problems with people or strange things that have been happening in your life in the past three months?"

She swallowed and began. "I was engaged to Stuart which began about three months ago, but about a week ago I ended our engagement when I saw him with another woman."

Dakota jotted down notes. "Anything else?"

"Yes. A couple weeks ago I started a coffee business with my Aunt Serena. She added half the money for the down payment and I added the other half. Only a few days ago, my aunt sent me a text telling me that the profit margins for the coffee shop were really low."

Sierra swallowed. "She warned me that if there isn't more profit soon, she wanted out of the business partnership." She sighed before continuing. "However, what I didn't know until recently, is that Aunt Serena hired Stuart to be the accountant for our coffee business."

Denver interrupted. "And I had a call yesterday from my private investigator Jake Davis. He said that from his investigation, he has reason to believe from documents he's found, that Stuart has been taking most of the profits from the coffee shop and making multiple small deposits, spreading them into different accounts."

Sierra gasped. "So, I was right. He is getting his revenge. Maybe he's the one who took my son."

Sheriff Turnbull responded. "Sorry, I just got a call from one of my officers who searched Stuart's house. There's no sign of your son. But we are looking into the documents and records Stuart kept in regards to your coffee shop."

Sierra nodded. "I'm glad."

Dakota continued to jot down notes. "All this information is very helpful."

Denver remembered something else. "I did get another call from Jake, about a topic that might or might not be related. He said they discovered the name of the teenager who was at Baxter's farm twenty years ago, on the day of the car accident. His name is Art Thompson."

Sierra's body stiffened and her eyes widened as she turned to Denver. "You said his name is Art Thompson?"

"That's the name Jake gave me."

Sierra swallowed and began speaking. "When I was reading my mother's journals this past week, my mother wrote that Art Thompson was the son my grandfather — Arthur Jeffries — had with another woman."

She paused remembering. "Her name was Laureen Thompson. My mom wrote that Art was the son my grandfather always wanted. My mom wrote that grandmother was very hurt that her husband cheated on her with another woman."

Denver sighed. "That is sad. But, it looks like the pieces of information that we need are coming together. Just ten minutes ago, Jake told me that Art Thompson confessed to cutting the brake line to that 1930s antique car that Sierra's parents John and Amelia Baxter were driving that day twenty years ago."

Sheriff Turnbull explained. "Well, in those old cars from the 1920s and 1930s if a person cut the brake line it affected the entire car. Nowadays cars are made a little differently."

Dakota questioned. "Did Art Thompson explain why he cut the brake line to John Baxter's car?"

Denver nodded. "He confessed that his stepsister Serena Jeffries told him if he cut the brake line of their car and John and Amelia Baxter died in a car accident, he'd get a third of the inheritance money that Serena expected to get from the death of her sister Amelia."

"However, Art said the joke was on him and he didn't

get anything. His stepsister Serena failed to realize that her sister Amelia already had her money tied up tightly in a trust for her daughter and son — Sierra and Eban Baxter."

Sierra's eyes widened. "So my Aunt Serena is behind all of this trouble — including being responsible for the car accident that caused my parent's death?"

"It's starting to look that way." Sheriff Turnbull shook his head sadly. "Do you know which trust Art Thompson is referring to Sierra?"

Sierra nodded and wiped a stray tear away from her cheek. "Yes. The inheritance that my mother left for me the day I turn twenty-five."

"And when is your twenty-fifth birthday, Sierra?" The crease deepened between the Sheriff's brows as he dug for answers.

"In two days."

Dakota nodded. "The timing of Sierra's son going missing is beginning to make sense now."

"What do you mean?" Denver questioned.

"Well, if Serena Jeffries wanted her sister Amelia's inheritance money badly enough that she was willing to cause a fatal car accident twenty years ago, it makes sense that Serena Jeffries would be willing to kidnap Cody now in order to get her hands on Sierra's inheritance money." Dakota explained.

"That's crazy and terrifying all at the same time." Sierra's face took on a tortured look. "My Aunt is responsible for taking my son isn't she?"

"I think so." Dakota spoke in calm tones and Denver squeezed Sierra's hand. "The thing is, we need to know where your Aunt Serena has lived or favorite places she likes to visit. Any place you can think of will be helpful."

Sierra nodded as if in a daze from all she had learned so far today. "Yes. About a month ago, my Aunt leased old man Erickson's Victorian house on the corner of Second Street. She still has the Estate left to her by my grandmother. It is located just two hours south of here just outside the small town of Andersonville."

Sierra spoke woodenly, as if in a bad dream. "The other piece of property that my mother wrote about in her journal is a small cabin at Emerald Lake. The cabin at the lake are only an hour west of Andersonville."

"Thanks. I think we have enough to expand our search. I have every expectation that we'll find your son, Sierra." Dakota's confident tone put a small smile on Sierra's face.

The Sheriff was already busy on the phone, calling the precinct in Andersonville and asking for a team to search the estate and to check out the lake house.

Denver held Sierra's hand.

He hoped this time the search truly would lead them to their son.

SIERRA COULD SEE the small two room cabin from the passenger side window of Denver's truck.

"Dakota is just ahead. He said to park on the dirt road and to walk quietly to the cabin. We don't want to alert your Aunt or Cody."

Denver's brother had asked Sheriff Turnbull to tell the

police officers to keep a careful watch on Serena Jeffries, but not to storm in and arrest her.

"It still seems weird that the police officers haven't arrested my aunt yet, since they know she has Cody here at the cabin with her." Sierra muttered hastily.

Denver parked the truck along the snow covered dirt road that was a short distance from the cabin. "My brother said he's seen a similar situation like this before where the kidnapper went a little crazy when the police stormed in and they killed the person they kidnapped. We don't want to take any chances."

Fear and anger knotted inside her at the thought of Aunt Serena doing something to harm her son.

Her hands clenched into fists as she thought of all the evil that her aunt had done to their family. Knowing that her Aunt Serena had deliberately planned the car accident that killed her parents was a heinous act of unbelievable proportions.

Now Aunt Serena — who Dakota had hinted might actually be mentally unbalanced — held her son.

It made her want to run to Cody to save him quickly, but she would heed Dakota's warning to wait for his signal.

As Denver helped her out of the truck, her body shook slightly. It was nearly noon the next day and she hadn't slept the night before.

She held onto Denver's arm, grateful for the comfort and support he'd given her in the last twenty-four hours. Sierra was aware that she had pulled away somewhat since Cody went missing.

Hiding had been her default ever since her parents

death in the car accident. Whenever something horribly wrong happened in her life, she mentally went inside herself as a safety mechanism. She was like a turtle who hid inside their shell to protect themselves from predators.

After they brought Cody home safe, she would need to apologize to Denver and explain.

Hopefully, once she explained and apologized he would understand. For right now however, the most important thing they needed to do was to protect their son and get him out of the hands of her hostile aunt.

Finally, they reached the cabin. Dakota walked just ahead of them. He motioned them to be silent and to follow him along the tree line that would take them closer to the lake.

They crept quietly along, the snow crunching softly beneath their boots, until they reached Dakota. They were hidden behind the trees.

Sierra could see Aunt Serena walking along the beach area, holding Cody's small hand.

There was only a little bit of snow on the beach. The water in the lake wasn't frozen instead it was lapping up against the shoreline.

She knew the lake water was probably freezing.

Her stomach clenched into a tight anxious ball at the sight of her baby. He had a bewildered look on his little face as he looked innocently up at her aunt.

Sierra wondered what lies she was telling her son.

She wanted to run over there to save him, but instead she waited for Dakota to speak.

"Okay." Denver whispered to Denver and to her. "You

see your aunt is walking with Cody along the beach. Sierra I want you to go out there by yourself to talk to her. Speak in a normal voice. Tell your aunt something like, you simply wanted to visit the cabin at the lake. That you have good memories of visiting this place with your mother."

He continued. "What we're hoping is that your aunt will keep talking to you, begin to relax and eventually loosen her hold on Cody. Then he will run to you and Denver and I and our police backup will close in and put her in handcuffs."

"You'll be here the whole time?" Sierra looked at Dakota and Denver, anxiety causing her to tense up.

"Yes. We will be watching and ready to run to you when you need us." Dakota's cool voice calmed her nerves.

"Okay, I'm ready." With a quick nod at the two of them, Sierra stepped out beyond the safety of the trees and towards her aunt and her son.

She reached midway along the shoreline of the beach, when Aunt Serena turned her head, surprised to see her.

Her eyes narrowed slightly. "Sierra what are you doing here?"

Sierra forced herself to relax and remain calm. She shrugged as she continued walking slowly. "I just wanted to visit the cabin at the lake that my mother loved so much."

"Hi Mom." Cody made a move to run toward her, but her aunt held tightly to his hand.

"Remember what I said, Cody?" Aunt Serena smiled but kept her grip strong. "You won't get that treat I promised you, if you run away from me."

Cody nodded, his face bewildered. "Okay."

Aunt Serena nodded. "Good boy." Her aunt's gaze studied Sierra. "Your mother never loved this place as much as I did. I was always the one who saw to it that the cabin was taken care of in winter and summer."

"It was the same thing with that large estate that was given to Sophie Anderson by her rich father, before she married my father, Arthur Jeffries."

Her aunt had a faraway look in her eyes. "Our shared mother left the estate to both of us, but I didn't think my stepsister Amelia would be able to take care of that large estate properly. So I made sure she wouldn't get the chance."

Sierra battled to hold onto her fragile control as her aunt confessed to getting rid of her mother.

"Now you're here. But, perhaps you knew you needed to be here. This is where you'll end and I will begin to take over control. I will control your inheritance money, the coffee shop and everything that's yours. Don't worry, I will see to it that everything is handled properly. See, it is fate. It's simply your time to disappear along with your son." Aunt Serena babbled on, not making a lot of sense.

Without warning, her aunt's voice changed to a sing-song high pitched voice.

It was almost like Aunt Serena had entered a different world in her mind.

"I don't know why you were able to keep your children Amelia, when our father forced me to abort my son. I'm going to go talk to my father about that. It doesn't seem fair that you have two and I have none. You've always had more of everything while I was given the leftovers."

Sierra swallowed the vivid fear churning in her belly. She looked at her son, who still didn't know what was going on around him.

She didn't realize that her grandfather had forced his daughter to have an abortion. That must have been heartbreaking for her aunt.

Maybe the trauma from that, had caused her mind to come unhinged? She didn't know. But she knew she needed to get her son out of danger.

Sierra took a step closer, forcing her body to stay relaxed.

All of a sudden Aunt Serena's voice became as high pitched as a little girl. "Come join us, Amelia."

Sierra realized that her aunt continued to believe she was her mother.

"Me and little Andrew are singing our favorite song." Aunt Serena began to sing in a sing-song voice a children's song about reaching the waves, touching the waves and riding the wave until the end of time.

Questions filled Sierra's thoughts. *Who was Andrew? Was that the name she would have given her son had her father allowed him to live?*

Her aunt's strange actions, caused fear to knot in her belly. She hoped there would be a moment to grab her son soon.

Aunt Serena sang and her and Cody began to step deeper into the water. She reached the highest notes of the song and continued to repeat the refrain.

When Aunt Serena lifted her hands in the air at the highest point of the song, she let go of her grip on her son's hand.

Sierra saw her chance. Motioning quickly with her hand towards Cody, she signaled for him to run to her.

It only took a moment for her son to realize what she was telling him to do.

Quickly, Cody ran straight into her arms.

Sierra grabbed her son in a tight embrace, while tears flowed down her cheeks. It hit her in that moment, that she'd almost lost him forever.

Footsteps crunched on the snow and she looked up to see Aunt Serena marching towards her with a determination and hostility in the set of her face.

Icy fear twisted around her heart at the sight of the hateful gleam in her Aunt's eyes. Sierra hurried to step away with Cody in her arms.

A rush of footsteps sounded loud on the snow packed lake front. Denver and Dakota ran toward Aunt Serena, grabbing her arms and pulling her away from Sierra and Cody just time.

Before long, Sheriff Turnbull arrived along with other officers and put handcuffs on her wrists.

As the police began to walk away with Aunt Serena, tears of relief flowed down Sierra's cheeks.

She embraced her son, holding him tightly like she'd never let him go.

Denver hurried toward her and wrapped his strong arms around both her and Cody.

"You're finally safe. I was so scared. I thought for sure I had already lost the two of you." Denver kissed the top of Cody's head and placed a tender kiss on Sierra's forehead.

His son softly whispered. "I love you too, dad."

DENVER'S HEART turned over as Cody said he loved him. And he adored being called Dad.

It wasn't that long ago, that he would have said that. But today, it was true.

He had been longing for the moment when his son would call him dad. Dreamed of it even.

But, he realized ever since his son was kidnapped, that he didn't deserve the title of dad.

The name dad was reserved for a man who kept his son safe.

In fact, as soon as his son went missing, Denver realized what he believed about himself during childhood was true. He would never make a good father. He was too much like his birth dad, who abandoned him and his mother when he was just a small boy.

The apple didn't fall far from the tree. It was certainly true with him.

The fact was, Sierra had kept his son safe all these years. And then in one night — after he convinced her that Cody should go on the hayride with other children — his son went missing.

What kind of horrible father was he who didn't know how to protect his own son?

His birth dad was a failure because he abandoned his family. Now he was a failure because his son was kidnapped.

He failed to keep him safe.

He failed to do the one thing that Sierra needed most — to protect her and her son.

Denver could tell Sierra was backing away from him. He'd sensed it already last night after Cody went missing.

In fact throughout the long night, she became more remote by the hour.

Until this morning, she wasn't speaking to him much.

She was scared and he understood that, but he felt the blame in her eyes when she looked his way.

He accepted that. In fact, he deserved it. He truly was the one to blame for their son's disappearance.

As he drove Sierra and Cody back to the Baxter's farm, he realized what he needed to do.

They got out of the truck and Denver spoke first to his son.

Placing his arm around his son, he held him close. "Be good for your Momma, son. She'll take good care of you."

"I will, dad. I love you." Cody hugged him quickly and ran inside the farmhouse.

Denver took off his cowboy hat and set it on the back of his truck and pulled Sierra into his arms. "I'm so thankful you're safe and that our son is safe. You're a good mother, Sierra. You will do right by our son all his life. I know that and I'm grateful."

He kissed her lips and held her close in his arms like he would never let her go. "All that matters now, is that you're going to be okay." He leaned closer and whispered. "I love you."

Denver embraced her, his arms gentle like she was made of glass.

"Did you mean it when you said you loved me?" Her eyes widened as they searched his.

"Yes." Denver leaned closer, taking in the sweep of her

lashes and the curve of her mouth. He bent his head to kiss her, needing one last taste of her lips on his.

Finally, he stepped back. "This is for you." He placed an envelope in her hand and squeezing her hand gently, he walked away from Sierra and got into his truck.

As he drove back to the ranch, Denver couldn't stop thinking about Sierra. He loved her. He loved his son. But, he'd almost lost them both.

His son had been kidnapped and almost died because of him.

He wasn't a good father. Which probably meant he would be a good husband to Sierra either.

Denver couldn't do that to Sierra. He wouldn't do that to the woman he'd come to adore.

He needed to be strong.

He needed to remind himself that Sierra and their son were better off — safer — without him in their lives.

SIERRA HARDLY SLEPT THAT NIGHT, even though she was exhausted from the day and night before.

Something troubled her about Denver.

There was such a finality to his actions last night when he had dropped her and Cody off at the farm.

When she opened the envelope, she'd read his intentions to buy out her Aunt Serena's portion of the title deed to *The Little Bean Cafe.*

He wrote that he wanted to buy the coffee shop and give it to her as a gift. That way she could run it debt free.

He'd also written a note. You deserve all the happiness in the world. Go chase your dreams, my love.

She tried calling him, but he wasn't answering his phone.

Sierra had this strange feeling that he was leaving again. She couldn't quite put her finger on it, but she felt it all the same.

Memories flitted across her mind from seven years ago.

She'd seen Denver the night before what was supposed to have been their wedding day.

He had been remote towards her then too. The kiss he'd given her that night, set her on fire.

Maybe that was his plan. Give her a kiss that would be fiery enough to last her for seven years.

Well, that wasn't going to work this time.

Sierra hurried to get dressed. She got in her car and drove towards Denver's ranch.

He had told her he was moving into the guest house as soon as it was ready. Maybe she'd find him there. If not she'd go to the Triple C ranch.

Either way, she was going to find him. She would get him to really listen to her this time.

Driving her old car, she turned onto his land, not stopping until she parked in front of his newly built guesthouse.

Denver's truck was still parked in the front.

The sun poked through the clouds with an orange red hue that seemed to set the sky on fire.

In the semi-darkness of dawn, Sierra trudged from her car to the door of the guesthouse.

With a firm knock on the door, she waited with a determination on the inside that surprised her.

The door opened suddenly and Denver's eyes widened at seeing her standing there.

"Sierra, why…"

"I'll tell you why I'm here." She walked into his house and took her shoes off. She also removed her jacket. She intended to stay awhile.

"Listen, I don't know why you're here but I was planning on…"

She interrupted with a smile. "Planning on flying out on the next flight and never coming back?"

His face paled a little and he ran a shaky hand through his hair.

His silence and the way he reacted to her accusation, only confirmed what she suspected.

"I don't understand why you would leave me and Cody? We were finally starting to respect, trust and love each other, now you want to leave?" Grief and frustration warred inside of her as she confronted him.

She stepped closer and put both hands on the sides of his cheeks, forcing him to look into her eyes. "Why, Denver?"

"Because, I'm not a good man for you to be tied to. I can't keep my son safe. I'm not a good enough father. Maybe someday you could find a man who will be a good enough husband for you and a good father for Cody."

A vein pulsed along the side of his neck as if holding raw emotions in check. "The night Cody was kidnapped should have proven to you that I can't protect you or my son." The green eyes that stared down at her were glistening with tears and misery.

"Ah, Denver. You think you aren't good enough for us?" Sierra's heart spilled over in her words. "You are more than good enough for me and for Cody. You have done your best for us and that's all anyone can ask. I don't expect you to be perfect."

"I don't want you to feel like you need to reach a certain level, before you are good enough to be a husband or a father. You are trying and doing your best, that's all that matters." She stepped closer. "You love me and you love Cody. That's what matters the most to me."

She wrapped her arms around his neck and kissed his lips. Denver's arms embraced her and his mouth covered her hungrily, like he was starving for his last meal.

He breathed a ragged breath and pulled back slightly just so he could look at her. "I tried to stay away from you, but I just can't. I still have so many fears that I won't be a good enough husband or a good enough father for our son."

"You've already suffered for the past seven years because of me and I regret that more than words can say. I love you, Sierra and I just want to do right by you." The vein in his neck was pulsating even more and his voice cracked.

He ran a finger along her cheek in a soft caress.

The despair she saw in his green eyes tore at her soul.

"I know you do, Denver. You are a good man. The best of men. You are more than good enough, you are just what I need and just what our son needs."

Sierra thumbs caressed the stubble along his cheeks.

"And the fact that Cody was kidnapped by my aunt, was not your fault. It just happened. Don't give up on us, Denver. Stay. You belong here, with us." Sierra searched his eyes and happiness filled her when she found a glimmer of hope and something more.

"I might need your help to find my way as a husband and father."

"We'll do this together, all right?"

A deep sigh resonated deep within him before he spoke. "Yeah, we'll do this together."

"Okay then." Sierra suddenly remembered the other thing she wanted to talk to him about. "But as far as giving me the deed to the coffee shop…"

"That was a gift. I've already contacted my lawyer to have him work out the details. I am buying the coffee shop and giving it to you because I love you. Not for any other reason that might be going through that beautiful head of yours."

Sierra smiled, needing to hear those words one more time. "You're doing that for me because you love me?"

"Yes" Denver's tender smile was nearly her undoing.

"Then, I accept your generous gift with overwhelming thanks." She looked up at him, her heart in her eyes.

"Good. I'm glad." Denver's eyes suddenly became serious.

Denver turned to reach behind him, grabbing a small box that sat next to a faded picture of her and Denver.

"You still have that engagement photo we took years ago." Sierra's eyes flew open wide as she stared at much younger versions of themselves.

They each wore matching baseball caps, her hair was

in a ponytail. The camera had snapped when they had turned to each other with sappy smiles on their faces. "

"That photo of us looks rather worn out."

Denver turned to her with a vulnerable look on his face. "That's because I've carried that picture of us in my wallet ever since I left town that day."

At his admission, her mouth dropped open.

Their eyes met and she felt a shock run through her at the force of longing and love she saw reflected there.

"You've carried this photo around for seven years?"

"Yeah. I thought if I couldn't have you as my wife, then at the very least I could have the memory of you to carry with me."

A stray tear slipped down her cheeks. Her heart melted into a warm puddle at his admission.

"Ah, Denver. You really do love me don't you?"

He gently rested his forehead against hers, his green eyes focussed on hers. "Yes. I love you with all my heart and have for years."

She sighed happily.

His hands shook as he held the small box in his hands.

"So, I was rather hoping we could make a change."

"What do you mean?"

Suddenly, Denver got down on one knee and opened up the ring box.

Her eyes flew open and one hand covered her open mouth at the brilliant marquis diamond she saw there.

"Sierra Faith Baxter, I love you with all my heart. Will you do me the honor of marrying me? This time forever?" As Denver's green eyes looked up at her, there was a new peace in his eyes, instead of that haunted look he had surrounded him.

"Yes. A thousand times yes!" Sierra placed her hands on both sides of his face and locked eyes with his, as her love for him nearly overwhelmed her.

Denver stood to his feet, grabbed her around the waist and twirled her around and around in the middle of the kitchen floor.

When he finally set her on her feet, he placed his hands on her cheeks and leaning down placed his lips on hers.

Sierra savored the sweetness of his kiss. This wonderful man who first inspired her to anger, now inspired her to love so very deeply.

Denver wrapped his arms around her. Sierra met his kiss with so many wonderful emotions rising up on the inside.

She could now look forward to the future.

With Denver at her side, she believed she could do anything. She could hope and dream again, knowing he would be there for her and she would be there for him.

They would build their dreams together.

CHAPTER FOURTEEN

A few days later...

DENVER STOOD at the front of the Community Church
listening to the joyful sounds of Church Bells ringing in
the bell tower in the background.

His hands flexed against the smooth fabric of his suit
pants as he tried to calm his nerves.

Deacon Miller played his guitar and crooned country
love songs in the background.

The Christmas Eve Church Service had just finished
and his wedding to the woman he loved had begun.

A tall Christmas tree shone brightly in the corner and
green boughs red roses and red ribbons adorned the
church pews.

Candles sat on candelabras and lined the front of the
church. Since the candles were electric and people didn't

worry so much about a fire hazard, candles were also placed along each of the pews.

The softly lit room sent out a warm, welcoming glow to everyone who arrived for the wedding.

Looking around the room, he noticed folks from different places. His music manager Sid sat next to members of his band near the front of the church.

On the other side his mom sat with a big smile on her face. She had waited for this day long enough. That's what she said, when he'd told his mom that Sierra had agreed to be his wife.

His older brother Wyatt, his wife Abby and their two boys along with his four younger brothers sat next to his mom.

Denver still felt a gaping hole in his heart from missing his dad. He knew his dad would have been thrilled to see him finally marry Sierra. Mack Callahan had said as much in the letter he wrote before he passed away.

As the Church Bells continued ringing, he remembered his Dad's last words and his last request that Denver give himself a second chance for love.

Denver looked at the angel that sat perched on the top of the Christmas tree, a reminder of the miracle of love.

You had the right idea after all, Dad. Sierra has always been my one and only love. Today she is becoming my wife. We have a son and now we'll be a family. I'm so grateful for a second chance that I really didn't deserve. So, if you are listening from up there today, I just wanted to say thanks.

A thoughtful smile turned up the corners of his lips. It was a good day to marry the woman he loved.

Reverend Jon stood nearby. He stood motionless as the

music played. Both were a calm source of serenity and peace, which was something he sorely needed today.

Even though he was used to crowds of people from years of singing in front of crowded stadiums, this day was different.

Denver recognized the significance of the commitment he was making and the gift of a second chance to marry Sierra.

He wasn't going to mess it up this time. No, this time he would do everything in his power to commit to her and love her like he should've done years ago.

Dakota stood next to him as best man and whispered. "It's time."

His brother had promised to let him know when Sierra stood at the back of the church, ready to walk down the aisle.

"Thanks." Denver grabbed his guitar and sitting down on the stool that had been setup near the microphone, he began to sing the song he'd written for Sierra.

Memories washed over him of the day he'd written this song. He'd been alone at a park watching an older married couple walk by, holding hands. Still loving each other after many years together.

It hit him like a fierce blow, how he had messed it up with Sierra. He wanted that forever kind of love with his one and only love.

Seeing Sierra standing dressed like a beautiful angel in the archway at the back of the church reminded him of his dream of a forever love with this incredible woman.

Long strawberry blond hair cascaded in waves to Sierra's waist like a glistening waterfall, making her look lovelier than he'd ever seen her.

She wore her mother's wedding dress and she'd never looked lovelier.

In her hands were simple red roses with baby's breath with a long red ribbon that hung down.

Denver watched her walk gracefully toward him now on Eban's arm with their son walking on her other side. He saw in her smile the dream of them together forever.

Today, he was pleased that instead of a stadium filled with fans as his audience, he would have an audience of one.

There was only one person he wanted to please today as he sang.

She was his one and only true love.

His bride, Sierra.

He began to sing softly, his eyes never leaving hers as she walked towards him in the dim candlelight.

"So many wasted years and wasted nights. So many years lost between us. Now, I only dream of you. I don't love nobody like you." His green eyes fixated on his incredible bride.

Last night he'd added new words to the song so he could sing them for his wedding day. *"I'm grateful for the second chance at love with you. A forever love that will last to the end of time. I don't love nobody like you."*

As Sierra began walking down the aisle, the words of

the song Denver sang were like an arrow piercing her heart.

She tightened her grip on her brother's arm and swallowed back emotion.

She passed by the folks from their small town smiling and excited to share this day with her and Denver.

The Peabody twins sat in a middle pew with rare smiles on their faces. Mrs. Moore and Mrs. Spaulding sat together and beside them were Ms. Hernandez and a few of the other people from the television studio.

Mrs. Lottie Jenkins grinned at her as pleased as punch, as did Denver's mentor Deacon Miller.

Grams sat next to Granddad who was in his wheelchair at the front of the church. They had both been so happy to see her marry Denver. They had been such a huge support to her since her parents died and she would be forever grateful for them.

Many more folks from town and ranchers from out of town had shown up to celebrate their wedding.

Sierra was grateful for all her friends and all their many blessings.

She was especially grateful to have her son back safely. The police had taken Aunt Serena into custody and had done some Psychiatric evaluation.

The Psychiatrist had diagnosed her with schizophrenia as well as a number of other mental disorders.

Sierra asked that instead of jail time, that her aunt be placed in a guarded mental institution where she could continue treatment.

When the doctor said it was all right to visit her aunt,

she planned to see her. After all, Aunt Serena was still her mother's sister.

Sheriff Turnbull, said they had found the evidence they needed to charge Stuart Gardiner with money laundering. It looked like he would face jail time.

Sierra was thankful justice was being done. Now, she really hoped that all the chaos of the past few months would be behind her now that she and Denver and their son were beginning a new chapter in their lives.

As she neared the front of the church and stood motionless as Denver finished singing the song.

Sierra couldn't help the tears that made their way softly down her cheeks as she listened to the last few lines of the song.

I'm grateful for the second chance at love with you. A forever love that will last to the end of time. I don't love nobody like you.

In her mind, as he sung the words to this song, it was his wedding vow to her. It was his commitment to be by her side, to help her and to love her forever.

Denver finished the song and they repeated the wedding vows to each other.

The moment Reverend Jon told Denver he could kiss the bride, he reached for her and put his arms gently around her waist.

Sierra's knees weakened and her pulse quickened as Denver's warm lips pressed against her own.

Her arms slipped further around his waist, holding tightly to her husband.

Love had melted her heart and turned her emotions into a messy puddle. She loved every second of it.

It seemed she had waited for such a long time for a husband who would love her like this. She had begun to give up, thinking it would never happen for her.

Denver really did love her and was committed to her.

She was going to have her dream of a family after all.

Now Sierra truly belonged to a family again. Not just the family she and Denver were making, but the large Callahan family as well. No longer would she feel lost and lonely.

Family was being restored to both of them.

Her heart overflowed with contentment and happiness.

Denver ended his kiss, his eyes flickering with a sweet tenderness.

Reverend Jon introduced them as husband and wife and the wedding guests clapped and cheered.

Denver grabbed Cody's hand and all three of them walked towards the back of the church.

Folks came to greet them and offered their congratulations. Even Mr. MacCrae stopped by and handed Denver an envelope, a mysterious smile on his face. "I'm quite happy to give this to you Denver."

The old lawyer cleared his throat. "As per your Dad's instructions, you've now completed all he asked of you. I'm sure he's pleased as punch watching how you've found your second chance at love. I'll be happy to see you begin more of those dreams. I wish you and Sierra every happiness as you start life together."

"What was that about?" Sierra asked after Mr. MacCrae walked away.

Denver smiled. "Just something my dad wanted me to

do after he died. This is a gift to the two of us from my Dad."

"Ah, that's really touching, Denver." Sierra knew what it was like to lose a parent you loved. "We will do our best to honor your Dad's gift to us."

Folks were mingling around them and Cody was with her brother, Grams and Granddad. They were taking him back to the farm tonight to give her and Denver time alone.

"Today feels like a restoration of all the lost years between us, Sierra. I'm so thankful for you."

Sierra nodded and smiled gently. "I feel the same way. We've been given a second chance at love and I'll be forever grateful."

Denver placed his hand on her waist and pulled her close. "Coming back to this small town was the best thing I ever did because it brought me close to you again. I love you."

A single tear rolled down her cheek at his words. She would never get tired of hearing him say those three little words.

"And I love you, Denver Callahan. With all my heart."

EXCITED TO READ DAKOTA'S SWEET ROMANCE STORY?
Grab *The Honorable Cowboy's Convenient Marriage* today.

She was so innocent, lovely and gentle — and the one woman that stirred his heart towards love. But he'd hurt her. Would he get a second chance to right old wrongs?

Now two years later, Dakota was back. To Sarah, this man was larger than life and twice as dangerous. She was worried that she would fall for him a second time. This time she feared, the heartache would be more than she could bear.

Dakota couldn't believe he was back. As he followed the trail of a missing child and her kidnapper, it led him straight to his home town. Worse, now he found himself on the mountain, hurt and in pain.

So, when the beautiful Sarah MacDonald finds him limping and in pain, trying to walk down the mountain, he chafes at having to depend on her for help.

Sarah insisted Dakota come to stay with her grandfather Angus MacDonald and her in their small cabin until he was fully healed.

When an angry man — a neighbor on the mountain — tries to force Sarah to marry him, Dakota steps in and offers the unthinkable... a marriage of convenience.

Trouble comes their way and Dakota has to use all his skills to keep Sarah close to protect her, while still protecting his heart.

Will being forced together tear Dakota and Sarah apart, or throw them towards true love?

ABOUT THE AUTHOR

Melody Archer lives in Southern Alberta with her husband and their four young adults.

Recently, her oldest son married his wife from Brazil and the whole family is having fun getting to know their new daughter-in-love. ;)

Melody loves new and classic romance movies, green smoothies and going on adventures with her family.

Melody would love to connect with you below. :)

facebook.com/memorablefictionbooks

instagram.com/memorablefictionbooks

bookbub.com/profile/melody-archer

pinterest.com/memorablefictionbooks

youtube.com/@memorablefictionbooks

ACKNOWLEDGMENTS

Thank you to all the wonderful people who helped me with this book.

To my cover designer, Wilette from Red Leaf Book Design, thank you for designing another gorgeous book cover.

Thank you also, to my proofreader Cathy who patiently read through each chapter, helping me make this story so much better.

A big thanks to all my wonderful Advanced Readers (my ARC reading team), who faithfully read and left reviews of this book.

Lastly, a huge thanks to my three young adult children who read through the manuscript, giving me all kinds of great suggestions on how to make this a better story.

Thank you everyone. I really appreciate you!:)

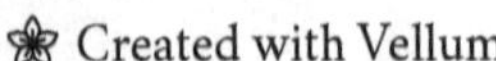 Created with Vellum